fiction by kōbō abe

NOVELS
The Ark Sakura
Secret Rendezvous
The Box Man
The Ruined Map
The Face of Another
The Woman in the Dunes
Inter Ice Age 4

SHORT STORIES
Beyond the Curve

PLAYS
Three Plays by Kōbō Abe

aroo

ook

*With the compliments
of
the author*

◆

The Publicity Department
Alfred A. Knopf, Inc.
201 East 50th Street
New York City 10022

Kangaroo notebook

A NOVEL BY

kōbō abe

TRANSLATED FROM THE JAPANESE BY

maryellen toman mori

ALFRED A. KNOPF   NEW YORK   1996

Kangaroo notebook

cleft-leaf radish sprouts

It should have turned out like any other morning.

I was munching on a crisp slice of toast, thickly coated with liver-and-celery pâté. I had one elbow pressed to the corner of an open newspaper; my upper body tilted slightly to the right. My eyes skipped here and there among the headlines as I sipped some strong coffee. I popped three tiny tomatoes into my mouth and squelched them together, for good health.

A tickling sensation ran up my shins. I rolled up one pajama leg and scratched. What felt like a thin layer of skin peeled off. Is it grime? I held it up to the light. It isn't grime or skin. It's scratchy, like dry beard bristle. Is it leg hair? Leg hair grazed by a flame would probably look like this, but scorched hair would give off a foul odor. I rolled up both pants legs and placed my feet on another chair, with my knees drawn up. There was no longer a single hair on my legs; if it weren't for the dotlike pores, the skin would have been smooth as a boy's. I had never had much hair, so I wasn't too concerned. Besides, with my pants on, the area didn't show.

Psychosomatic hair loss? That could be. Head hair probably isn't the only hair that falls victim to stress.

Around three months earlier, a "suggestion box" had been installed at the office, and all employees were required to propose a new product twice a month; just an idea would do. Anyone whose proposal was chosen would receive a substantial cash reward. I hardly expected to receive a reward, but since I had to submit something, half in jest I scrawled a note and stuck it in the box.

It was just one phrase:

Kangaroo Notebook.

That was all.

But lo and behold, my scribbled note was chosen. I received a memo from the Product Development Office asking me to report. The manager himself met with me.

"That sort of thing is no good. It was just a whim. It's not worth taking seriously."

"Quite the contrary! I suppose you have a rough sketch?"

"I just happen to be interested in kangaroos. . . ."

"And that's fine! I'm fond of kangaroos too. The image is good and the word has a nice ring to it. A good idea is catchy!"

"It's the kangaroo's ecological traits that intrigued me."

"So the gist of your suggestion . . . in short, just what is kangarooish about the notebook?"

"When you put it that way . . ."

"There's a pocket somewhere, right?"

"Just last week there was a magazine article called 'Marsupial Pathos' . . ."

"That reminds me, aren't koalas marsupials too? Wait a minute—come to think of it, my son's shoes are called wallabies or something. Wallabies are related to kangaroos, aren't they? They have a certain charm, those marsupials!"

"According to that article, 'Marsupial Pathos' . . ."

"In any case, I'd like it by this weekend. A rough sketch will be fine. . . . Naturally, mum's the word outside our department. . . . If it's accepted you'll get a bonus, of course, possibly even a raise. . . . I'm counting on you!"

"But, getting back to marsupials, the longer you observe them the more you realize how pathetic they are. As I'm sure you know, marsupials and higher mammals have parallel evolutionary branches that mirror each other: cats and dasyures, hyenas and Tasmanian devils, wolves and Tasmanian wolves, bears and koalas, rabbits and bandicoots. . . . Pardon me for digressing."

"If you see you've derailed, you should get back on track." Obviously his adrenaline was flowing; his smile had shifted to a furrow between his eyebrows. "I want to hear what's behind your suggestion."

"For instance, at the zoo, why are the koalas so popular?"

"That's it, go on!"

". . . Take the stripes on a squirrel's back, for example. Besides being well-defined, each stripe pattern is unique. But a phalanger's stripes are indistinct, and it's virtually impossible to tell one pattern from another. And a marsupial mouse is quite nimble, but it's no match for a real mouse. It would seem that marsupials are poor imitations of full-fledged mammals. Their inadequacy gives them a certain appeal; we're touched by it."

"Just what are you getting at?"

"It's nothing, really. . . ."

I can barely recall how I managed to escape from the Product Development Office. I went to the toilet and vomited about a cupful of stomach acid. After work I stopped at a beer hall and order a medium stein, some sausages, and a plate of pork dumplings, but I detected an odd yeasty smell, and I couldn't bring myself to touch anything but the beer. As the liquor took effect, once again a flush spread across my shins. When I rubbed the areas with the palm of my hand, they felt rough, like a fresh cucumber. Has a strange change occurred in the pores of the shin hair that came out this morning?

I went home, immediately took off my pants, and examined the areas. Not only were they rough, but a black dot the size of a poppy seed protruded from each pore. When I pressed, there was no pain. Neither was there any sign of festering or internal hemorrhaging. Is it clogged grime? In the shower I scrubbed briskly, but it made no difference. The bumps seemed to be just a normal enlargement of hair roots that preceded the growth of new hair.

In my dreams appeared sketch after sketch of nebulous notebooks, each with an infinite number of pockets within pockets.

"Generally, a notebook goes in your pocket, doesn't it? Give that notebook its own pocket. . . . In that pocket, put another notebook. . . ."

T h e   n e x t   m o r n i n g I woke up while it was still dark. My legs were unbearably itchy. I spread a thick layer of antihistamine salve on each of them. The black particles in the pores were over twice as large as they had been the night before. On closer inspection I saw that they were not mere bumps; beneath each black dot was something that looked like a plant's stem. Like bean sprouts, only finer. Their plantlike appearance was odd, so I tried plucking one. Instead of staying whole, it tore, and some liquid oozed out.

I peered at it through the magnifying glass on the handle of a letter opener. It does seem to be a plant. There's a stem whose tip flares out like a primary leaf. If it were hair, it would just taper toward the tip. I was dumbfounded by the thought that it might be a plant.

I had a quick breakfast of yogurt with honey, then left the house. I seemed to recall seeing a sign for a dermatology/ urology clinic somewhere behind the district office building. I knew it was too early, but I couldn't sit still. Contacting the office to tell them I'd be late could wait until after I'd had a preliminary examination.

I found the clinic right away. Both the building and the neighborhood had a secluded, run-down feeling about them. It's probably the sort of place that a patient with a venereal disease would appreciate. The circumstances are ideal for discreetly undergoing treatments.

There was a sign at the entrance:

"New patients may register after 7:30 a.m. Indicate if your case is an emergency. Otherwise, please return at the time stated on your appointment card."

Apparently their clientele isn't limited to patients who slip in surreptitiously. The way real estate prices are skyrocketing, even a doctor with a thriving practice probably has to settle for a back steet office if he wants to do business ethically.

To the right of the clinic was an apartment that had been converted into a nursery school, and to the left was what seemed to be a warehouse for aluminum materials. The neighborhood was still completely silent. I sat down on the steps of the nursery school, rolled up my pants legs, and shuddered. Not even an hour had passed, but the scaly areas on my shins had changed visibly. Perhaps because of the higher body temperature and humidity there, growth in the places closest to the knees was proceeding most vigorously; the stems beneath the primary leaves had taken on a faint but definite color. I've seen this plant before. Why, this might be a "cleft-leaf radish sprout." That's one of my favorite vegetables; I eat it once every three days, dabbed with mayonnaise.

When I realized what it was, my anxiety turned to fear. I felt like screaming and rushing around. It was six forty-five. Unfortunately, it was still more than half an hour till the clinic opened. But I have a rare affliction; I'm an emergency case! Surely I have a right to ring the bell and request a special consultation!

Through the window I had seen someone moving around. I could restrain myself no longer. I pressed the bell at the front entrance. There was no response. I continued to press it, but whether it was broken or was disconnected, it didn't seem to ring. I pounded on the door with my fist. Nothing worked.

"Be quiet!" said a thin female voice, then the door to the entrance was finally unlocked. It was past the designated time.

"It's urgent."

"State your case when the reception desk opens. If you have a high fever or you're in extreme pain, the appointment order will be changed. . . ."

A girlish woman in a red gown vanished coldheartedly behind the reception counter. She was wearing glasses that were round as the eyes of a damselfly.

"I don't have a fever and I'm not in pain, but I have a bizarre condition."

No response. I stooped down and peeked through the window at the low counter and saw Damselfly pinning on her nurse's uniform cap and blotting her lipstick with the edge of a tissue. She ignored my pleas and slid me a plastic card that said "No. 1."

"After all the patients with appointments have finished, you'll be first. Let's see, you probably ought to come back around eleven o'clock."

"But doesn't the sign say to indicate if your case is an emergency?"

"An 'emergency' with no fever or pain won't do."

"I have 'radish sprouts' growing from the pores of my legs."

"You have what?"

" 'Radish sprouts.' "

"You're joking."

"It's the truth. Here, I'll show you."

I rolled up my trouser cuff and raised my ankle onto the counter. It was a ludicrous posture, but I was dead serious. The "radish sprouts" were developing even more lustily than when I had inspected them on the steps of the nursery school. By now, no one who saw them could dismiss them.

"Can I remove one stalk? I'll go show it to the doctor. He's still eating, but . . ."

"I wonder if it'll kill his appetite?"

"Possibly."

I must say, she was a credit to her profession. She carefully wiped the area of my shin with alcohol and wielded the tweezers adroitly. "Now, if you'll pardon me . . ." On this unexpectedly formal note, she pulled one stem. It tore off midway.

"Sorry. Did it hurt?"

"Not really."

"Maybe I shouldn't have turned the tweezers. Will you let me take one more?"

This time, how gingerly the delicate fingerwork. How serious the eyes behind the round spectacles. The curve of her eyelids is startlingly lovely. Beneath that gaze my "radish sprout" disease seems all the more wretched and ugly.

One stalk yielded to the tweezers and slid out with a slippery sensation. There was no pain or irritation. On the contrary, I felt relieved, as if a boil had been lanced.

"It's a 'cleft-leaf radish sprout,' right?"

"It looks like one, but we'll have to ask someone like a greengrocer to verify it."

"That red bead on the tip of the root might be blood, don't you think?"

"I'll go show it to the doctor."

"Ask if he'll please examine me right away."

"No fever, right?"

"Fever or not . . ."

"Sit there and wait."

The nurse disappeared behind a shelf of patients' charts. I quickly rolled down my pants cuff and lowered my leg to the floor. The joint in my groin ached from maintaining that unnatural pose.

The entrance door opened and the first patient rushed in. An elementary school student with a scab on his ear. The second patient was a female junior high school student with a brilliant red inflammation around her mouth. No sooner had the door closed than another patient dashed in. To my surprise, most were schoolchildren. None of them misbehaved; each one went to the shelf, picked a comic book, sat down on a bench, and began turning the pages. Then one by one came young women, until a little group had assembled. Cosmetic rash, burns from cooking oil, and so on. My assumption that the clinic's sequestered location meant that it catered to VD patients was evidently due to my skewed outlook. Yet I sensed something suspicious and hostile in the way the female patients stole glances at me. I'd be relieved to be suspected of harboring gonorrhea. If they knew I was cultivating "radish sprouts" on my shins instead of hair, how in the world would they react?

From the examination room came the squeaking of a swivel chair. It seemed as if hours had passed, but according to the clock it was only six minutes and twenty seconds.

"Patient Number One, this way, please."

The nurse's thin, sweet voice. I dashed toward the examination room door and bumped into the boy with eczema on his earlobe.

"Look out!" The kid kicked me in the shin. It didn't hurt, but I instinctively yelped. The nurse opened the door, took the child's arm, and whisked him inside.

"Wait for your turn."

"But my card says 'Number One'!"

"People with appointments have priority. I told you that, didn't I?"

"But it's an emergency. What did the doctor say? You showed him, didn't you? What you just removed?"

The nurse placed her hand on the child's back and pushed him behind the door.

"Pull yourself together. At a clinic, aggravating the nurse won't help your cause."

"I'm sorry. I didn't mean to. What did the doctor say? Did he agree that it's a rare disease? Isn't this sort of thing unusual?"

The sound of throat-clearing. Just beyond the door, six feet away at the most. The doctor.

"Is it that 'radish sprout' fellow?"

"He's out of control. . . ."

When I overheard this, I stopped breathing, and my back tensed. For the other patients to get wind of my condition would be disastrous. Fortunately, the doctor has a low, husky voice; it probably doesn't carry to the waiting room.

I made my appeal through the slightly open door.

"Do you know of other cases like this? Is there any cause for alarm?"

"I've just sent my wife to the greengrocer's for confirmation. You know, many skin conditions are caused by fungi, and a fungus itself is a kind of plant, so . . ."

"Well, that's true. I can understand that. But among higher plants, are any parasitic?"

"I'll have a close look at it later."

The nurse placed her soft, slender hand on my chest and pushed me back. "Patients who exaggerate their conditions are the ones we loathe."

Already the benches in the waiting room were completely full. I decided to phone the office. Maybe it's better to take the day off than to go in late. After all, I have "radish sprouts," not athlete's foot. The area below my knee was gradually swelling. I leaned against the wall and waited. I never imagined dermatology clinics to be such bustling places.

It was afternoon before all the patients with appointments had been seen. I marveled anew at my perseverance. The nurse opened the door with an innocent smile, and at last I was granted admission to the examination room.

The doctor came out of the lavatory and whooshed into the room like a cyclone, his white gown flapping. He sat down on the swivel chair and stretched. A middle-aged woman's voice pursued him from somewhere in the back.

"Do you think it's safe? Since we don't know . . ."

"Nonsense." He greeted me with a sheepish, crooked grin that didn't match his flat-nosed, dauntless face. "Sorry to keep you waiting. It's the children's allergy season. I can't even find time to eat. Well, let's have a look at it. . . ."

The nurse tapped the edge of a clothes basket and said, "Pants here, okay?"

The doctor took one look at my leg, let out a gasp, and rose from his chair.

"My word, this is extraordinary; why, it's practically a jungle. . . . It's only on your leg, isn't it—this parasitical growth?"

"Did the greengrocer think they were 'cleft-leaf radish sprouts' too?"

"What the greengrocer thinks is just a layman's opinion. . . . It's dreadful, that much is certain. . . ."

I instinctively stood on tiptoe, as if to distance myself from my legs, if ever so slightly. During my several hours in the waiting room, the plant's growth had steadily accelerated. The sprouts closest to the knee were developing most rapidly. The stalks were about a half-inch high, and from each of them a two-fold leaf had neatly opened; the foliage was so dense that the skin beneath it was already concealed. Strangely enough, even though they had not been exposed to the sunlight, the leaves were a fresh vegetable green.

The doctor straightened up in his chair and sighed deeply. I couldn't tell if he was pondering my condition or trying to put some distance between us. He began coughing and wheezing and waving his hand emphatically.

"To bed!" he commanded.

Then he crouched over the trash container at his feet. It was a stainless-steel container with a foot pedal for opening and closing the lid. The nurse began leading me over to a nearby examination table, but the doctor shooed us away and snapped, "Not that one! The one for surgery!"

"This way!" ordered the alarmed nurse, and guided me

to the door. Behind us the doctor had begun to vomit. He sounded like a cat with a bone stuck in its throat as he vomited on and on.

T h i s   o p e r a t i n g   r o o m   is strange. . . . It was a garage-like enclosure with raw concrete walls that had not even been finished with mortar, much less tile. Moreover, the room was lower than the hallway by about two steep steps. One wall consisted of iron roll-up shutters. There was no window anywhere. The only light came from oversized fluorescent lamps on the ceiling. If not a garage, then it seemed like a torture chamber. The bed was the one high-quality piece of equipment. It was a sturdy iron piece, with guardrails on either side of its thick mattress. Its entire surface had an ivory finish. At the head of the bed was a control panel with a row of various switches. Maybe dermatology and urology operations require special equipment. . . .

"Your jacket and shirt go here. . . ." Keeping her distance from me, the nurse pushed the clothes basket next to my bed.

"I wonder why the doctor was throwing up."

"Take your clothes off and lie down. Here's a blanket. Put the thermometer in place."

"Are my legs all that grotesque?"

"Just between you and me, Doctor had 'radish sprouts' in fermented soybeans for breakfast today."

"That's a shame. . . ."

Again I was kept waiting for a long time. I didn't look at the clock, but at least an hour must have passed. I even dozed off. I awoke when the nurse gripped my arm. She wound a piece of rubber around my upper arm, then swabbed alcohol liberally on the inner elbow joint. The thermometer had already been removed.

"May I draw some blood?" Answering such questions is meaningless here. "Pardon me."

I didn't feel any pain. These days injection needles are disposable, so they seem to pierce more cleanly. Besides, my veins are thick as earthworms, so it must be hard to botch the job.

I became drowsy again. Maybe drawing blood was just an excuse to drug me. I slept soundly. I woke, drank some juice by my pillow, then drifted into another sound sleep.

I didn't know how many hours had passed. I didn't even know whether it was day or night. I tried to move, but it was impossible. My arms and legs were tightly strapped to the bed with a synthetic-rubber belt. Not only that, a stainless-steel pole stood beside my right ear, and hanging from it side by side were a large vinyl bag bulging with pale-yellow liquid and a fist-sized transparent bag. The two tubes which ran from these were joined by a connective device into a single tube that was stuck into a spot just beneath my collarbone.

I faintly recalled a conversation between speakers I could not identify.

"I wonder if this is a bit insecure."

"Should we make an incision and insert it directly into the vein?"

"Here, let me do it."

Everyone is smiling. Everyone is kind to me.

"A kangaroo notebook jumps out, warm from inside the pouch . . ."

"Your urine is passing through a tube inserted in your

urethra. . . . Yes, it's fine; it will automatically collect in the bag down below."

"I don't like it. It's like urinating once inside, then sending that urine to the outside. . . . I don't like this sort of thing. . . ."

It's probably night. The sound of wind. The distant moaning of the wind, like a test signal on a radio.

"Before debating whether or not these are 'cleft-leaf radish' sprouts, shouldn't we first of all resolve the question of what a 'cleft-leaf radish' is? According to the investigation conducted at my request, there is indeed such a thing as a 'cleft-leaf radish.' However, since a certain firm in Shizuoka Prefecture holds the product patent—one might say it's a corporate secret—its true identity is a complete mystery. The company claims that it is a variety of the 'twenty-day radish' and that they import the seeds from the state of Oregon so as not to cause trouble for Japanese radish growers. The problem is that during laboratory testing, despite our painstaking efforts, the sprouts refuse to grow into radishes. As soon as we transplant them to the earth, they begin to rot. I wonder why in the world that is."

"Maybe among plants it's a kind of marsupial."

Time seems to be standing still. I want to eat some cotton candy.

The wind is singing "farakumba, merakumba, clarakunda . . ."

Strangely enough, there was not a single completely dark spot in the room. Maybe it was because of the two large fluorescent lamps on the ceiling. It was not exactly "indirect lighting," but the electric bulbs themselves were not visible. The light from the lamps was amplified by skillfully placed reflectors so that the location and the direction of the light sources were concealed.

That light dimmed slowly. Why? Maybe for no reason other than to conserve electricity. The door seemed to keep opening quietly. On the floor, a circle of light from a flashlight. Someone creeping around the foot of the bed, then the rim of the light circle grazing my forehead. I quickly shut my eyes and pretended to be asleep. It seemed like the right thing to do. The person with the flashlight flipped a switch on the wall near the floor and pushed up a lever beside the shutters. The shutters began to roll up with a screech. Evidently the person wasn't tiptoeing to avoid waking me up. Suddenly I opened my eyes and glared. A sharp beam of light pierced my eyes, so I couldn't tell who was there.

I tried to communicate the fact that I had no wish to cause trouble, that I was the soul of tranquillity, but I couldn't find my tongue and I seemed to have forgotten how to talk. When the shutters were half open, the individual with the stealthy steps approached and peered at me from directly above. It was the doctor. I could not hide my mild disappointment that it wasn't Damselfly.

"I asked the nurse for some ice water."

That's what I meant to say, but I couldn't have said it. My voice would not come out. Oddly enough, I received a response.

"Unfortunately, she's only here during the day. Besides, your liquid intake is being supplemented by the intravenous drip, so there's no need to worry. Starting to feel bored?"

"Not at all. I'm perfectly content. The 'radish sprouts' on my legs are bound to clear up soon. This sort of thing can't last long. Maybe I'll try putting some in my miso soup tomorrow morning."

"I'm sorry to say that your case is beyond me. I've discussed it with various specialists I know, but . . ."

"Are there any? Specialists?"

"There aren't."

"I thought not."

"You don't mind?"

"No. Because I've put myself in your hands."

The doctor's face grew smaller and smaller. It receded toward the ceiling. It fused with the ceiling and turned into a sprinkler. Is this an hallucination? From the start I knew there was a sprinkler. It's a slightly eerie sprinkler that looks like a human face. At the same time, it's the doctor. Somewhere along the line, reality and illusion seem to have merged. Or have they? Isn't there a theory that an illusion which one realizes is an illusion isn't a true illusion?

The sprinkler smiled and murmured apologetically. "I've come to the conclusion—and this is a terribly old-fashioned view—that in your condition hot-spring therapy is the only hope. Preferably a sulfur spring, the most potent one possible."

"Like Hell Valley . . ."

"Exactly, like Hell Valley . . . assuming there's an inn willing to take you in . . . those legs of yours aren't likely to make a good impression on the other guests. . . ."

Slowly the bed began to move. It was as if I had willed it and, at the same time, as if it was beyond my control.

"Don't take it personally. Dawn is coming, so do watch out for cars!"

T h e   b e d   i t s e l f was incredibly sturdy, and heavy too, but its wheels were small, so I didn't expect it to move smoothly. But when it actually began moving, it seemed to be gliding. Maybe it's propelled not by mechanical but by psychic power. No, that's absurd. I'm not so far gone as to expect spiritual energy to perform physical work. Recently at factories and such I hear they're using air cushions in vehicles that transport heavy objects. This bed was made by the Atlas Company, the number-one manufacturer of hospital equipment in the world, so apparently it's in a class of its own when it comes to high-performance precision functions. It's equipped with every feature imaginable—electric, continuous reclining; a sixteen-hour battery that operates during power failures; a wireless alarm system on the head panel; an oxygen mask that's activated automatically in emergencies . . . But this is strange; how can I know so much about hospital equipment? Am I just imagining all these things? If not . . . This is a more dire possibility, but am I actually a medical equipment salesman, and have forgotten this? There's no making sense of it. Anyway, all I know is that this is an Atlas bed, and it seems to be capable of moving in response to my mental commands.

The bed's maneuverability was not that great, and it was hopeless in terms of speed. It crawled along and turned awkwardly. That was probably partly because I hadn't yet perfected my psychic ability to convey my wishes. Maybe once I had developed some skill, I would be able to steer it more accurately and to regulate its speed. I concentrated my psychic energy in the center of my forehead, visualized "motion," and left the clinic garage.

I didn't know exactly what time it was, but because the clinic was on a back street there was hardly any traffic, and of course no pedestrians. I coasted slowly along the sidewalk. Behind me, the sound of shutters closing.

"Thanks for everything."

I couldn't move my body enough to look back. I sniffled. For some reason, a strangely sentimental mood swept over me.

I had no particular destination in mind, but I decided for the time being to go west, since the road in that direction was somewhat downhill. I could conserve energy. A young woman came toward me at a trot; she stared suspiciously at the bed, looked up at the IV pole, and just glanced at my face. Well, that's understandable. If I came across an invalid hooked up to an IV who was gadding about in a self-propelled bed, I'm sure I'd steal a glance while pretending not to see.

My next encounter was with a man who looked flabbergasted and made a mad dash for the sidewalk across the street. He cocked his head and ran off shaking his torso, as if trying to assess how drunk he was.

A taxi passed. It did not even slow down.

I cruised around the city for a while, strapped to the iron bed. Before long I realized that going up and down curbs consumed more energy than I had expected. It was a nuisance, so I decided from then on to boldly join the street traffic.

I turned the corner at a tall building and was assailed by a sudden gust of wind. My terry-cloth blanket blew up from my feet. I was chilled to the bone. I tried to cover up my legs again, but the restraining belt prevented me. What a mess. I don't mind the cold so much as the fact that the "radish sprouts" flourishing on both my legs are fully exposed. Passersby won't be as tolerant as they've been until now. I've suddely metamorphosed from a poor invalid into a monster. Otherwise-indifferent passersby might be seized by a lynching impulse and beat me to a pulp.

In the wind, my legs began to freeze. Are the "radish sprouts" absorbing my energy and impeding my ability to retain heat? If only I could move my right hand. I mustered as much psychic energy as I could and tried to guide the bed out of sight. Maybe I tried too hard; the bed sideswiped the curb, and one leg landed in a gutter. After that, it wouldn't budge an inch.

S o m e o n e   g r a z e d my face with a beam from a flashlight. Relief welled up in me. It must be a doctor or a nurse. I've finally awakened from this interminable nightmare. But unfortunately it was neither a doctor nor a nurse. Instead of the fluorescent lamp on the ceiling, a large, industrial-sized flashlight. In place of the sprinkler, a white helmet. A man in uniform, shaving his chin with an electric razor, was looking down on me. His eyes showed signs of a hangover; they were still red and watery.

"This is hazardous. In another hour you'll be obstructing trucks going in and out."

Now that he mentioned it, I realized that I was in front of a construction site. Thick nylon netting stretched around an iron scaffolding. The man was probably a security guard on patrol.

"I'm not here for the fun of it. . . ."

My voice is back! I can feel my tongue again, and I'm moving my lips as usual. The anesthetic must have worn off. I can move my head back and forth a little. If I'm just careful of the IV tube, I can move my right arm from the elbow quite freely. Did the doctor loosen the belt before throwing me out?

Sensation in my legs had also begun to return. The terrycloth blanket that had flipped up in the wind had at some point resumed its proper position.

"You're seriously ill, aren't you? If there's someone you'd like me to contact, just let me know."

"That's out of the question. I don't think I can rely on anyone's help anymore."

"You haven't been abandoned, have you?"

"I guess I have."

"There are some pretty heartless people out there. I suppose it was the hospital staff or your family. . . . This IV bag is nearly empty, you know."

"It looks like I'll just have to die."

"Cut that out. Who should I contact? For illegal parking, it's the police. For oversized garbage, it's the district office. For lost invalids, it's the fire department. . . . It all depends on your pride."

To tell the truth, I want to go back to the dermatology clinic behind the district office building. No doubt they treated me shabbily at the end, but I feel I had a sort of rapport with that bony nurse wearing the round glasses. Even the doctor and I might have seen eye-to-eye if we'd just had a little more time.

But instead of just turning me out, they chucked this expensive bed along with me. They say that when a mother abandons her child, the more precious the items she leaves with it, the firmer her resolve.

Enough of this! I'm acting like a milksop. The best course of action is to simply wait for the IV solution to run out, then shrivel up and die along with the "radish sprouts."

The guard smoking a cigarette at the foot of the bed suddenly raised his voice in surprise.

"Hey, there's a luggage tag here. Maybe you're a kind of mail parcel." He shone his flashlight on the tag wired to the bed leg. "You were about to be sent to some sulfur spring. Something or other 'Hell.' I can't read it; the ink is smeared. . . . So you must be a piece of lost property. Anyway, I'll phone a police box for you."

The sky lightened slowly. Today, too, a thick, solid mass of clouds hung low in the sky; I couldn't very well expect the "radish sprouts" to wither naturally. A large insect struck the nylon net noisily and got lodged there. It looked like a cicada.

The guard came trotting back. A big concrete mixer stopped nearby at the side of the road and gave a short honk on its horn. The guard responded by blowing his whistle; then he rolled up the net. The trapped cicada dropped off like bird dung. It was probably dead. The driver of the concrete mixer eyed me suspiciously, and then, without displaying further interest, drove into the construction site. The guard rested against the side of my bed, leaned toward me, and while lighting a cigarette, he began whispering to me.

"See this? It's a fake Dunhill lighter. They call it a Dunvale. They say even a pawnbroker wouldn't know the difference. The cop at the police box is contacting a patrol car right now. I guess he received an alert bulletin about you. They

CHAPTER TWO

the chartreuse poet

enty minutes had passed since I had been
and all, down the mine shaft. Something like
irming around under the bed. Is that the bed's
rce? We kept on going.

le we careened down a steep incline. The bed
like a rat undergoing electric shocks. It's a won-
n't crash into a wall. Is this bed equipped with
aticollision device? That's hardly likely. Even the
Atlas bed wouldn't come with features totally un-
asic function. No, it's more likely that there are
into the floor of the tunnel that are acting as

might treat your case as illegal parking. 'Illegal parking' is a strange way to put it. I'm always baffled by what government offices do."

In the pale morning light, I saw that the IV bag was already flat. It had a reddish tinge, like an old dried squid. My time is running out too.

A patrol car came to an abrupt stop. Behind it was a small truck carrying a crane; on its side was written "Tow Truck." A middle-aged police officer wearing an ordinary uniform cap got out.

"This guy?"

"Thank you for coming." The guard, looking pleased with himself, returned his salute. The officer removed some postal-sized cards from a slim document file and held up one of them to me.

"Can you see this?"

"Yes."

"You look exhausted. Do you know what this is a picture of?"

"I do."

"Tell me."

"A pig."

"That's right, it's a pig. But isn't there something funny about it? Isn't the most important thing missing? I wonder what it is. See if you can tell me." He pressed the button on a stopwatch.

I noticed it right away. The pig had no tail. It was just a rough sketch made from a single line. A crudely drawn pig was sticking out its head over a crudely drawn trough. What was the point of the cop's interrogation? Whatever his intent, it was obvious from the start that he was trying to make me answer "the tail." I became furious. If the man had admonished me for the "radish sprouts" on my legs, I might have reacted more meekly. But this was intolerable. It was an affront to my honor. I perversely began searching for flaws in the sketch of the pig.

"Well, let's see now. This pig is facing a trough and poking its head out, but its head's at the wrong angle. It'll starve to death this way. Do you suppose there's a defect in its optic nerve? What's more, you can't see its tongue. Since it's opening its mouth so wide, its tongue ought to be sticking out. If it doesn't even have a tongue, it will certainly starve to death. No, I understand. Of course, you're trying to make me say 'the tail,' aren't you? If I say, 'The tail is missing,' I'll pass the test. But it's out of the question. I believe you said 'the most important thing.' A tail can't be so precious to a pig. Even with its tail chopped off, if it had the urge to copulate it could perform splendidly. To my mind a well-functioning optic nerve and tongue are far more crucial. You can plead all you want, but you won't get me to say 'the tail.' "

The policeman pushed the button on the stopwatch, nodded, and jotted something in his notebook. I thought I would be commended for my keen powers of observation, so I began to feel thwarted as I waited in vain for some reaction. Then, in a perfectly businesslike manner, the man began speaking into his radio.

"Sixty-six seconds. Cooperativeness is zero. I'd put his resistance index between seven and eight."

He raised his hand and motioned to the tow truck.

"What are you going to do?" I asked. But no one would answer me anymore. Because of the IV tube stuck beneath my

It would take years for gutters to be hollowed out of concrete. Maybe unknown to me, hundreds, or even thousands, of iron beds are roaming around the streets like stray dogs every night. Where they come from and why they're out wandering around is a mystery, but roving beds might not be such rare creatures. Maybe every time the police receive word of a bed sighting, they dispatch a wrecker to seize the bed and dump it down this mine shaft.

The wheels screeched and the bed bounced. A sharp pain spread slowly through the area beneath my collarbone where the IV tube was lodged. Has the adhesive bandage come loose? Am I bleeding? This darkness is frightening. I want light.

My bladder had received a severe jolt too. While the intravenous fluid in the bag was steadily decreasing, the bag of urine was swelling like a bullfrog's belly and was about to burst. Has my urine reversed course? The discomfort of wanting to urinate but being unable to is no laughing matter. When I was in junior high school I had a homeroom teacher who suffered from an enlarged prostate. One time, a sudden early-morning attack of anuria sent him to a clinic. He rushed around the building frantically, waiting for it to open, and finally, beside himself with agony, he stuck his head into a Y-shaped iron decoration on top of the fence and killed himself. Cruel youth that we were, we treated the incident like a huge joke, a memory that now fills me with shame.

There was also a change in the motion of the bed. The erratic bumping had turned into smooth, regular rocking. Controlled rolling, double-beat rhythm ringing at regular intervals . . . thanks to that big bounce, did we land on actual rails?

It's too good to be true. Even the rails of a narrow-gauge

railway wouldn't match the width of a bed. Oh, if you searched you might find a pair that fit. . . . The ones for those miniature trains driven by monkey engineers that you see at amusement parks? Or for handcars in mine shafts?

Come to think of it, while they were unhooking my bed from the wrecker, the workmen were whispering to each other:

"Smells like sulfur, huh?"

"It's hydrogen sulfide."

There's a coincidence, isn't there? If the place expecting me is a sulfur mine, then these rails must be for the handcars that transport sulfur ore. Didn't the urologist say that? As a treatment for "radish-sprout" disease, the only thing I can think of right now is a sulfur spring. The staff's way of doing things wasn't exactly cordial, but I guess I can't complain. Apparently I'm being transported according to the instructions on the doctor's chart.

The regular rhythm created by the track's joints had a hypnotic effect on me, like nostalgia. A dream of falling through a hole into another, deeper hole. Wait a minute! That could be a useful image! A hole inside a hole. There's a hint of obscenity about it; it might be just right for the kangaroo notebook. I want to jot down some notes. I have to get hold of something to write with as soon as possible.

A beam of light!

Even though my eyes were closed, my retinas responded sensitively. I had to open my eyes, even just a slit, and look. Someone was testing my pupils' reflexes with a flashlight. I peeled my tongue off the dry roof of my mouth and implored the person whom I could not even see:

"Please, give me some water. Look, the IV bag is practically empty. . . ."

The flashlight went out. I could see the ceiling. That sprinkler with the human face. The fluorescent lamps that were cleverly designed without covers to provide indirect lighting just by using reflectors. Nothing has happened. I'm still on the table in the operating room. These realistic dreams are bad for your health. I'm totally exhausted.

"When the time comes, it's changed."

I realized that indeed the IV bag had already been changed. A bag with brilliant red goldfish that these days you see only at festival booths.

"Excuse me. I seem to have a bad case of motion sickness."

"Autointoxication, I suppose—by those 'radish sprouts.' "

My ear was reflected in the nurse's round glasses. They seemed to be plain glass.

"Can I please get some medicine for seasickness?"

"I can't give you anything that's not on the chart."

"But this rocking is terrible, isn't it?"

"Roll up your sleeve. I'm going to draw some blood."

"If it were an earthquake, it would be more than magnitude five."

"Let me measure the length of the 'radish sprouts,' okay? Pardon me."

The terry-cloth blanket was rolled up. The nurse's seemingly jointless fingers began groping through the luxuriant patches of "radish sprouts."

"That tickles!"

"It feels so lush. These must be plenty nutritious."

I seem to be having an erection. This is awful! The last thing I need in my condition is an erection. In the first place it's embarrassing, and besides, with a catheter in me, it might severely damage my urethra or kidneys. Think of something else and distract yourself.

The perfectly precise rhythm produced by the track's joints.

> *Farakumba, merakumba, sarabunda*
> *Rub it in red pepper oil*
> *Wrap it in banana skin*

The verse slipped out naturally, like a refrain. It was non-sense, but it went well with the rhythm of the rails. The nurse giggled.

> *Farakumba, hanakumba, hanabenda*
> *Rub it in red pepper oil*
> *Wrap it in banana skin*

I chanted with increasing vigor, and finally I even added a melody, like the jingles sung by little girls as they bounce rubber balls. It was masochistic, yet exhilarating too, and my singing grew all the more impassioned. Maybe because of that passion, the nurse's smile slowly melted. The contours of her round glasses gradually blurred, then the glasses receded toward the sprinkler face on the ceiling. When they reached the sprinkler, they turned into old-fashioned black ebonite glasses. Then the face looked just like my father's. I realized that it was just a sprinkler, but at the same time it was definitely my father. My father was a small, top-heavy man with a frisky gait. For reasons unknown to me, he had lived apart from my mother for years. So aside from his thick-heeled polished cordovan shoes and the horn-rimmed glasses that he claimed were tortoiseshell, I can't remember anything about him.

All this time the bed continued to race along. The pulsating sound, the flow of the wind, and, above all, this incessant vibration. Yet there's no doubting the fact that somehow, someone replaced the old IV bag with a new one. Which situation should I declare "real" and which one a "dream"? To rid myself of the parasitical illusion, I focused all my energy and tried repelling what was above my closed eyelids. The sharp pain of an electrical discharge. The human-faced sprinkler immediately took flight.

Within ten seconds, I came face-to-face with, not a sprinkler, but an ordinary lamp. It was one of those orange sodium lamps that you often see inside tunnels. Roughly every thirteen seconds we would draw up to one, then pass it. It was an extremely monotonous, endless ride.

Farakumba, clarakumba, sarabenda . . .

The song of the rails gradually grew plaintive, tapered off, then subsided.

To pass the time, I plucked a few "radish sprouts" and munched on them. That fresh, slightly tangy, homely, radishy taste. The only thing missing is salt. I licked my sweaty arm. The trace of saltiness cleared my throat. One's own perspiration isn't disagreeable.

To ease the tedium, how about challenging myself to a little quiz? A mental game will help pass the time.

Problem: Based on the time interval between two lights, compute the speed of the bed.

Too simple? Assuming the distance between lights to be sixty feet and the time interval between them to be approximately thirteen seconds, the speed of the vehicle is . . . First of all, divide twenty-five by thirteen and find the speed in seconds . . . $25 \div 13 =$ . . . This is absurd! How can I do such a calculation without paper or pencil? A scalpel raced through my head, sharp as a high-frequency dog whistle. Maybe arithmetic problems aren't good for "radish-sprout" disease.

I took several deep breaths and threw myself into counting the joints on the track. . . .

Three thousand six hundred and six . . . three thousand six hundred and seven . . . I was interrupted by a shaking, accompanied by subterranean rumbling . . . Three thousand six hundred and eight . . . A train coming from the opposite direction? It hardly seems likely, but it gives me an uneasy feeling. I raised myself up on my elbows, awkwardly craned my neck, and squinted hard. Thanks to the row of lamps, I knew that we were approaching a curve. Visibility was poor, so I couldn't see far, but I made a critical discovery. This is a single-track railway! We're bound to crash any minute!

The rumbling was getting closer. Soon it filled the entire tunnel, as if the space had been plugged with a cork. It sounds like five ten-ton trucks. Is it a caravan of handcars loaded with sulfur ore? If we collide, the bed and I will be smashed to smithereens. I prepared for the worst; I urinated with all my might and gripped the IV tube with my right hand.

An intermittent, shrill warning whistle. Headlights smoothly drawing open a curtain of light.

That doctor's chart—what a joke! He must have left it blank from this point on. I don't want to end like this. I wish he'd at least told me the name of the sulfur spring.

Violent rocking. I was resigned to crashing, but we just managed to avoid it. Fortunately, there must be further instructions on the chart. We switched from one track to another and were shunted into a side track. I'm drenched in sweat. Fine, this sweat will come in handy later as "radish-sprout" seasoning.

A small, five-car vehicle whizzed past within a hairsbreadth of the bed. Because of the dust cloud raised by air turbulence, I sneezed several times in a row. Something's really odd. What went past wasn't the handcars, as I expected, but a brightly decorated miniature train, the kind you see in amusement parks. Especially the garish designs painted around the windows. Those must have been done with noctilucent or fluorescent paint; despite the strong color-filtering effect of the sodium lamps, they looked plenty gaudy.

Is that music? It sounds like a circus brass band, or a popular song, or maybe just the wind. . . .

At any rate, it was a very peculiar train. Miniature trains in amusement parks often operate by remote control. So if you don't see an engineer or a conductor in the train, you're not surprised. And if it's after hours, naturally there are no passengers. But what if there's just one passenger? That's mysterious and disturbing. The little girl waving her hand through the window of the back door of the second car. . . . Her way of waving bothered me. She was six or seven, ten at the most. Was she just being playful, or was she frantically trying to communicate something? Those long, sloping eyes that looked as if they were about to run down her face . . . She was pressing her cheek to the window and staring out wide-eyed. Was she smiling or terrified? I still can't figure that out.

Beneath the bed, the soft whir of flywheels rotating. We slowly began returning to the main track. Maybe for a while there are no trains scheduled to come from the opposite direction, so there's no need to rush. That train carrying the little girl, where was it headed? Usually, miniature trains in amusement parks keep going around and around in a loop. The place where my bed was dumped must have been either the end of the line or its starting point. Was the miniature train trying to get back there? Or did it miss a switching point somewhere? One possibility is that people have become sick of the miniature train, and my bed has been chosen to take its place on the loop as a novelty. Special exhibit at a health fair: the world's first "radish-sprout" patient. Instead of being taken to a sulfur spring, maybe I'll just keep being paraded around the fairgrounds until my entire body turns into a "radish-sprout" patch. . . .

There's a more optimistic way of looking at it. How pleasant to imagine that miniature train as a special vehicle for transporting patients home after they've been cured of their afflictions at hot-spring spas. Even the sloping-eyed little girl who was waving at the window may have been on her way home from a health resort where she was being treated for touch-me-not growing on her shins. Come to think of it, she was an adorable little girl who probably had an enchanting smile. Since I had a chance to look at her, I wish I'd paid more attention to the shape of her mouth.

The monotonous ride continued.

For vitamins and fiber, I munched on some "radish sprouts." I gathered a thumb-sized bunch of sprouts from one patch, taking care not to create any bald spot; a lopsided haircut is unsightly. I wiped some sweat from my side, licked my fingers, then nibbled on the leaves. I'd prefer soy sauce, but I can't be choosy. I ate the stalks only out of a sense of duty.

There was nothing to do until we arrived at the hot-spring spa, so I closed my eyes. I dozed off, how long and how soundly I couldn't tell. I woke up briefly, then drifted off again.

D a m n i t , I'm starving! I'm sick of vegetables! I want starch or protein, I want pork dumplings or noodle soup!

I wonder how long I've been sleeping. I can't even tell if it was one hour or twenty-four hours. I've had it! This sense of restriction is intolerable.

The bed kept whizzing along on the rails, but it seemed as though the headwind had grown stronger. Has the incline just become steeper, or are circumstances changing?

An odd, viscous odor in the wind. Is it sulfur? No, it's different from sulfur. It's much more organic, like the odor of underground malls. After office hours, when the flow of water sharply decreases, the sticky odor of sewage fills the malls beneath city buildings. The chief component isn't sulfur, but ammonia. They say that sometimes the rats can't stand it and come staggering up to the street. Of course, up there old stray cats are waiting to welcome them.

Sudden curve. Sudden stop.

The sound of water lapping against an embankment. It was slightly painful, but I raised my upper body and twisted my neck to the right. The IV tube was digging into my right collarbone, so it was hard to turn to the left.

We were at the end of the tunnel. An underground canal, covered by a huge arch, was blocking our way at a right angle. Probably in the past it had been a river used by barges, but as transportation facilities developed, it was turned into a culvert and used as an outlet for rainwater and such.

The rails terminated abruptly on a pier-like structure. Here my bed waited patiently for something. Maybe a ferry will come to meet us. The canal water was black and stagnant, and it was smooth enough to see the ceiling lights reflected in it. A narrow walkway with an iron guardrail. A green emergency telephone box. A blue signboard with white letters that seemed to give the name of the city or else the store located directly above. Unfortunately, it isn't bright enough to make out signs on the opposite bank. If I hold my nose and breathe through my mouth, the place has a bit of the atmosphere of a canal city.

Something that looked like a small pig, smeared with tar, went floating downstream from right to left. Can it be a plump kangaroo? Waves rippled slowly across the surface of the water. Only the creature's head protruded above the water. It's the skeleton of a mammal, but it's impossible to tell what kind. Its jaws are completely different from a human's. Since it's not a human, I suppose I'm not obliged to report it.

The waves gradually narrowed in width. Has a boat come? The quiet creaking of an oar being plied. The sound of water slapping against a boat's side. If that doesn't sound exactly like the introduction to Pink Floyd's "Sorrow"! The piece was recorded by the new group that formed in 1987 after Roger Waters left because of a dispute among the band members. I was a longtime fan of the horsey, clean-shaven Waters, so maybe I was a bit prejudiced against the piece. But the introduction is steeped in the mood of earlier times, and it's not bad. Someday, if I'm given the chance to return home, I want to listen to all their songs again.

From downstream, suddenly a small fishing boat appeared at the opening to the tunnel. An oar was moving at the boat's stern, but there was no oarsman. A screw-type automatic rotational device isn't especially unusual, but it must have been difficult to design a reciprocal-motion device like an oar. Why was it necessary to go to such lengths? The only reason I can imagine is that the noise of the screw was considered undesirable. Is it a spy boat charged with some special mission?

The boat turned slowly toward the end of the pier and began to approach it. The front of it was flat, and it was roughly the same height as the pier. On its deck were rails whose gauge fit the bed's wheels. They were just under ten feet long at most. It looks like this is the ferry that's come to pick me up.

I wonder if the miniature train that passed, carrying the sloping-eyed little girl, also transferred at this pier? The boat's docking device latched onto the pier. The bed began moving forward cautiously. When the bed finished boarding the boat, the docking device popped open, the draft was lowered, and the boat left the shore. The draft line dropped more than I had expected, and each time waves hit, the deck was drenched. I bent my knees and wrapped the terry-cloth blanket tightly

around my legs. It would be terrible if the "radish sprouts"—
my precious food supply—were contaminated by the canal water. The boat turned around and headed downstream. Apparently the main function of the oar was to steer; it was just
quietly floating on the water.

The boat was about twenty-five feet long. It had no sails,
but there were tall masts in the front and back. Rope entwined
with electric lines stretched between the masts. It looks like a
squid-fishing boat that's been converted to a ferry. In the middle of the boat was an opening with a roof over it. Inside was
a ladder for going down into the cargo space. Using my ab-
dominal muscles as little as possible in order to protect my
bladder, I called at the top of my lungs: "Is anyone there?"

The structure of the overhead arch seemed to amplify the
echo effect. My voice diffused into meaningless sound as it
bounced back and forth between the walls, and became a shout
that reverberated like the blare of a Tibetan trumpet.

We continued downstream with the flow, the boat's oar
quietly creaking. Sometimes there was a sign or a stone staircase with a banister where it seemed a boat could dock, but
my boat kept clear of these, as if from a sense of hostility.

There was one sign I could make out, thanks to its plain
writing and because it was right beneath a light.

$$\boxed{\text{M I K K A D Ō}}$$

Something squirmed in my memory.

"At that moment the man was savoring a chocolate parfait
on the second floor of the Mikkadō."

That's it! I'm sure this is the first line of a suspense novel that left a deep impression on me. It's called *The Daikoku Bombing Incident*.

It was one of three books of my father's that were sent to me by parcel post four years ago, after his death. The other two comprised a pharmacological experiment manual, one volume on organic matter and the other on inorganic. It was a specialist's reference work in which no one would be interested unless he was planning to poison someone. I had time on my hands back then, so I ended up reading *The Daikoku Bombing Incident* three times.

I had no obligation toward my dead father. My parents had lived separately for a long time, and my mother had died five years before him. Who had sent me my father's belongings and for what purpose, and, above all, what the sender's intentions were, I had no idea. In any case, a legacy was a legacy. I couldn't very well pitch what I'd just received into the garbage. As I riffled through the pages of the novel, I noticed my father's writing here and there, so my curiosity was aroused.

The first half of the book was a pretty preposterous adventure story. But the second half included a commentary entitled "The Chartreuse Poet," written by the author's friend. This essay played a role in proving the innocence of the author, Phinny Fleetfin. I think there were things that made one suspect that the novel's author and the close friend who wrote the commentary were actually the same person. My father was so convinced of this that he noted it in the book. (I myself am in full agreement.)

In his story, the author, Phinny Fleetfin, was warning of

a bombing in a cleverly disguised way. In those days the Dai-koku was a luminary among new department stores that were posing a challenge to old, established shops, so it had captured the attention of the stock market. Naturally, this novel that had dared to use a real store's name immediately became a best-seller. Of course, it was just a novel; no bombing actually oc-curred. But this practical joke was suddenly treated as a true story when some mischief-maker caused an explosion by tossing a timed waterproof firecracker into the canal (which at that time, before it had become a culvert, was apparently utilized by the lumber industry at Kiba).

Newspapers and radio broadcasts openly referred to Phinny Fleetfin as a criminal, and it was rumored that the po-lice, too, though they were more discreet than the media, were conducting an investigation of him. One reason the author was so strongly suspected of foul play was that at the time of the firecracker incident, Fleetfin was in fact a frequent customer at the Mikkadō, which is right next to the Daikoku. The author of "The Chartreuse Poet" made the superficially persuasive claim that Fleetfin had behaved in the same way as his main character so as to gain the experience he needed to write a convincing story, and not to case his intended crime location. But on this page my father had made a question mark in red ink and had penciled in small letters: "A criminal always re-mains attached to the scene of his crime."

Of course the close friend did not rest his defense of the "chartreuse poet" at this rudimentary stage. Everyone he knew who had even once beheld the poet's wistful smile was con-vinced of his benevolence. His gaze, suffused with the innocent light that radiated from his pure soul, and his voice, like a balm that soothed life's stings, naturally endeared him to men and women alike. There were those who disapproved of his womanizing, but it was young women who were constantly making advances to him; why should he be held accountable?

It was just envy, jealousy, resentment. . . . But our "chartreuse poet" had other troubles. In the first place, he suffered from chronic gallbladder inflammation. That greenish countenance which captivated women was no mark of divine favor; it was merely a symptom of bile backup.

This disorder contributed to further misunderstanding of the man. In patients with chronic cholecystitis, blood circulation in the internal organs is sluggish. After eating, they have to lie down immediately for at least thirty minutes; for an hour if they have consumed a lot of greasy food. The blood's entrance to and exit from the liver must be kept at the same level, or the person's bilious complexion will turn ashen, then florid. If this happens, the condition can even prove fatal.

One time, after eating at a noodle shop, Fleetfin immediately went to lie down on the second floor. The woman with him misinterpreted his behavior as a sexual advance, and proceeded to strip from the waist down and mount him. Another time, right after leaving a high-class restaurant, he just said to his female companion, "Give me thirty minutes," and plopped down on the road. The gorgeous creature, who was dressed to the teeth, was mortified beyond words and ran to the police to report him. When you think about it, the cause of all the misunderstanding, misplaced jealousy, and so forth can be traced to Phinny Fleetfin's doleful chartreuse face. It behooves all women to reflect on this and recognize the existence of love that seeks no return.

At this point Father had written in, "Hogwash! It doesn't make a bit of sense."

Evidently my father wasn't as interested in Phinny Fleetfin's love affairs as in the notorious *Squid Bomb*.

The Daikoku Bombing Incident was published in the 1920s. That was way before I was born, but the gloomy age of censorship had apparently already begun. It was mainly the passages in the book that dealt with the squid bomb that my father had covered with his notes in red ink. According to Fleetfin's research, if you sun-dry the sexual organs of a male and a female squid and bring them into contact at the rate of three hundred fifty feet per fifteen seconds or less (the average running speed of a third-year junior high school student), you'll create an explosion surpassing dynamite.

In the novel, the motive for targeting the Daikoku isn't entirely clear. But the tale's account of the development and use of a bomb made from a living creature apparently created quite a sensation. All over the country secret experiments were performed, and my father's marginal notes seemed to suggest that he too had somehow been involved in such experiments. Certainly in those days inciting others to commit acts of violence was no less a crime than engaging in them oneself.

The author of the commentary asks rhetorically at the end, "Which of them ought to be held responsible—Fleetfin the Squid Bomber, or the Chartreuse Lady Killer?"

It was a crafty way to conclude his defense, but unfortunately I didn't believe a word of the novel. One of my father's worthless possessions had given me a glimpse into his agitation, and I had derived a few driblets of amusement from it. That was all.

R i g h t   a f t e r   I   p a s s e d   the Mikkadō sign, the IV bag at the top of the pole began blinking in a slow rhythm—once every two or three seconds—and emitting the pale light of a firefly squid. According to *The Daikoku Bombing Incident,* this blinking is a vital condition for detonating a squid bomb. Of course, the novel is talking about squid, not IV bags. It's not as if any pair of male and female squid will do; some squid respond to each other and some don't. As the two squid are brought together, their blinking must become more and more intense. The reason that *The Daikoku Bombing Incident* ended in failure and that the experiments and research which it inspired did not succeed may well have been that the importance of this male-female compatibility factor had been underestimated.

Naturally, I don't believe any of this. How could I possibly believe it? Besides, this is an IV bag, not a squid. Even so, I can't be completely nonchalant. It's begun sending flashing signals somewhere. I jiggled the IV pole and removed it from the bed rail. I laid the pole between my knees and examined the bag; it was blinking at about the rate of breathing.

This is bad. It's the worst-case scenario. At some time or other the plastic bag was switched with what is obviously organic matter. This is a squid. These are squid organs that look just right for sashimi. I wonder when the switch took place. I don't know how to tell male from female, but judging from this blatantly seductive writhing, mine must be the male.

The female squid organs seem to be drawing near. My squid is twitching more and more lustily. For decades the novel has gone without a successful conclusion; can it be that all conditions are finally satisfied and the novel is approaching completion? It's too unfair. I'm just a reader.

Right beyond the sign for the Mikkadō was a U-shaped terrace that seemed to have once been used as landing area. An eleventh-hour strategy. Somehow I've got to get on shore before the female squid catches up with us. Once on land, I'm home free. How the organs of the female squid manage to make contact with those of the male unfortunately isn't detailed in *The Daikoku Bombing Incident.* Squid may have soaring power, but when two of them leap out of the water, they can't possibly perform such a feat as instantly bringing their reproductive organs precisely into contact. Of course, the one who planned the bombing of the Daikoku Department Store was either the novel's author or one of his characters; squid themselves don't harbor such ambitions.

I should unburden myself so I can take on any sort of enemy. I've removed the IV pole from my bed, so my upper body is freer. Next, chuck the urine bag. I didn't dare pull the catheter from my urethra, so I decided just to take off the bag. I pulled it up from the side of the bed. It was heavy. It seemed to weigh as much as five volumes of an encyclopedia. Whether from the dirty canal water or urine that had leaked, the bottom of it was soaking wet and it felt horrible.

Because of the echo, I had no sense of distance, but from somewhere outside my own boat came the sound of an oar creaking and water splashing against the side of a boat. Maybe because of the fog, visibility was worse than I'd realized. I glanced back and forth across the surface of the water. It was relatively easy to see reflected light moving on the waves. Blobs of light, like melted jellyfish, rocked on the water about midway upstream. Is that it? When I squinted I could make out what, sure enough, seemed to be the shape of a fishing boat. It's closer than I expected. At most, three hundred yards; timewise, that means five or six minutes. I have no time to lose.

Thinking I'd separate the urine bag from the catheter, I located the joint, then tried yanking it and turning it, but it wouldn't budge. The tube wasn't screwed on or inserted; it seemed to be attached with glue. What a nuisance! Holding the heavy bag in my left hand, and in my right hand clutching the stainless-steel pole from which the squid was hanging, I moved my hips for the first time in a long while. Even though it was very loose, the belt that restrained my hips was in the way. I thought I'd undo the buckle, so I let go of the stainless-steel pole. A sharp pain. I shrieked. I forgot about the tube lodged beneath my right collarbone. Is this tube still necessary? Even if I can't get rid of the urine bag, I can probably easily rip off the squid organs. It's hardly likely that they're supplying me with nutrition. So I thought, but I hesitated. There's no telling what trouble might arise if the balance between myself and the squid is disrupted. After all, my life is full of unexpected events these days.

With the pole in my right hand and the urine bag dangling from my left, I climbed down from the bed. Unaccustomed walking. This is what humans were meant to do. Unfortunately, the deck was drenched in dirty water. The "radish sprouts" on both legs rubbed together, as if I were wearing midcalf fur boots. The damp boots felt unpleasant. I faced the stern and observed the fishing boat that was pursuing us, carrying the female squid. I had no point of reference, so my estimate wasn't precise, but the boat's outline had become quite clear and it seemed to have covered half the previous distance between us. Like my boat, it appeared to be driven by an automatic steering device. That thing hanging from the mast in the boat's bow must be the female squid organs. Pale fluorescent light blinking. It even synchronizes perfectly with the rhythm of my squid. The two are responding to each other. The "chartreuse poet's" prediction was on the mark.

I released the crank from the oar at the stern and switched to manual operation. Fortunately, I had some rowing experience. Keeping a set distance between my hips and the urine bag, I changed direction, pointed the boat at what appeared to be the dock at the Daikoku Department Store, and began paddling with all my might. Whether incited by the sound of my oar or by an instinctive agreement between the two squid, the boat in pursuit turned starboard and began to press in on us.

I'll be standing on the corner of the dock. When the female squid gets close enough, I'll thrust out my stainless-steel pole and strike it down. But my docking technique was inept. With both hands encumbered by large baggage, I slid down between the dock and the boat. A sharp pain, as if my urethra were tearing. Fortunately, my right elbow, which was clutching the pole with the squid, caught on the dock. I somehow managed to scramble up. The pain in my penis might subside before long, but my "radish sprouts" are irrevocably contaminated.

Before my eyes was an old, concrete flight of stairs. From the canal it had been hidden in the shadow of a pole and I hadn't seen it. There was a crude plastic signboard with red arrows and a store's name written on it.

> VARIETY SHOP
> WORLDLY DESIRES

It was a popular store that occupied a corner of the Daikoku Department Store. The shop sold its merchandise through a mail-order catalog that I subscribed to. The catalog, called *Worldly Desires,* had "Worldly" written with a Chinese character and "Desires" in romanized Japanese. If I heard the word "Worldly" I would immediately think of the Daikoku, but the reverse was not the case. No, the first thing that sprang to mind when I heard "Daikoku" was Phinny Fleetfin's book. Suddenly I wanted to drop by the Worldly Desires shop. That seemed, more than anywhere else, to be the sane world. It was the land of childhood, where humans and objects intermingled. It was a fetishistic world, where the boundary between spirit and matter dissolved. Even the persistent female squid could not possibly penetrate that territory. The Mikkadō, where Phinny Fleetfin or his fictional alter ego had once savored a chocolate parfait, had long since changed hands and become a toy shop specializing in video game software.

The direction of the wind must have shifted; suddenly the foul odor intensified. The boat giving chase was now within fifteen feet of us. As I suspected, there's no crew. How in the world does it intend to trigger the blast? Without any hesitation, it went into action. The female squid's organs, which until then had been dangling from the mast like a sample at a fish market, began to flash like a small strobe and to swing like a lure toward my squid. This is quite a performance. Obviously, I've underestimated it. I fended it off with the hook on my pole. The metal hook gouged into it, making a squishy sound. The female organs spun around in midair and rebounded like a yo-yo. What happened next was more appalling. My squid organs twisted and leaped up, their anger evidently aroused. That jerking on the tube sent a sharp pain through me, as if my collarbone had been torn out. Oh, now I get it. Just because you're my squid doesn't mean you're my ally. Squid have their own common desires. The "chartreuse poet" hit upon exploiting the explosive power of those passions for terrorist purposes.

Now I'm scared.

This is no time to vacillate. I want to escape into the Daikoku Department Store. Into the city and the lifestyle of ordinary human beings who have nothing to do with self-propelled beds, underground canals that aren't on the map, and doing battle with squid organs. But it's out of the question, isn't it? For someone with "radish sprouts" growing on his shins, that's asking too much. Should I just tear down the male squid organs and toss them into the canal? No, it's too risky. I'm dealing with something entirely different from fireworks, which can't tolerate moisture. After all, this is a sea creature. It could very well cause an explosion in the water like a tornado. And if it does, my number's up.

Was my destiny predicted by the "chartreuse poet" over thirty years before I was born? But he didn't mention the "radish sprouts" on my legs. Was the vegetable not yet being produced in the 1920s?

The female organs mounted their second attack. Using my

urine bag as a shield, I somehow managed to prevent the pair from making contact. Urine that had leaked from pressure began to spread out in concentric circles on my briefs. On the end of the stainless-steel pole, the male organs squealed and blew bubbles. This is too much. Maybe it's time to act. If I take long steps, it's at most five paces to the staircase of the Worldly Desires shop. I used the pole hook to drag the blanket over from my bed.

Of course, this is hardly the proper attire for a department store customer—blanket wrapped around my waist, a bag of urine in my left hand, and a metal pole with squid organs dangling from it in my right hand. If I blunder I could incite a riot. But even this getup is probably safer than a sports shirt, urine-stained briefs, and bare feet. At least the blanket will hide my "radish sprouts."

Besides, I don't intend to hang around the Chanel counter. Nor do I plan to stroll around the food section, helping myself to free samples. I just want to take a quick peek at the Worldly Desires shop. In a place like that, there must be plenty of self-centered customers who aren't stifled by bourgeois values. A keener interest in trinkets of self-adornment than in people is a symptom of alienation.

Before the third attack began, I dashed for the stairs. They were covered in slippery moss, as if they hadn't been used for years. Behind me, the enraged shrieking of the female squid sounded just like a pheasant in heat. My male squid began twitching spasmodically on the end of the pole. It's a stud pig trying to mount an elephant. But the pulsing light assisted me in climbing the dark stairs. I rested the heavy urine bag, which was digging into my fingers, against my knee. On the landing

I switched it to the other hand. At the place where I'd stopped climbing, there was an iron door on which something barely legible was written in white paint. Fortunately, the door opened, creaking noisily. I made it! Stairs again. The squid had stopped flickering, but since the moss was dry, it was actually easier to climb the stairs than before. Thanks to a small naked electric lightbulb, I could decipher the characters on the next iron door: "B2."

An explosion of light. An office, storage area, and staff dressing room all in one. Terribly elegant Baroque music coming softly through speakers. I rewrapped the pale-pink blanket securely around my waist. With each step I took, water dripped onto the vinyl floor.

Luckily, I made it up the last staircase without meeting anyone. There was no iron door here. Right behind a plastic screen engraved with a peacock design was the store. There were very few customers, probably because it was midmorning. I caught the glance of several clerks. Actually, as soon as our eyes met, they looked away. It was probably an expression of anxiety rather than courtesy to a customer. Only one person persisted. He watched me constantly out of the corner of his eye. Thin, well-groomed mustache, dress shirt with pale-green vertical stripes, Art Deco necktie setting off a fashionable collar.

Feigning nonchalance, I immediately began perusing the merchandise at the watch counter. Then I moved on to the next counter, novelty items. A computerized fortune-teller . . . a pig that changed colors with the weather . . . a machine that spat out lottery chips . . . a penis sheath made in New Guinea . . . a radio made in 1907. . . .

Right now, what I need are shoes, trousers, a fresh shirt, writing utensils, a Swiss army knife, a small pocket flashlight. But the dandy in me was drawn to the attaché case corner. Most customers who frequent this sort of shop are after a watch or a briefcase.

Along the way I passed a sporting goods section, where a pair of chic jogging shoes caught my eye. They were black and gray, with snazzy red lacings. I picked them up and was glancing at the price tag and the writing on the rubber soles when I heard a voice.

"Excuse me, sir, but have you come without your wallet?"

It was the man with the mustache.

"My wallet?"

"That's right—your wallet."

Of course. One needs money to buy things. If not money, then a credit card. Stunned by my own absentmindedness, I glanced around. Many people were watching to see how things would turn out. Some quickly averted their eyes, but the rest continued to stare unflinchingly.

"Now that you mention it, I left it in the clothes basket at the clinic."

"Allow me to escort you to your office."

Under ordinary circumstances, he probably would have gripped my arm at that point. But he seemed hesitant to touch my shirt, which was dank, dirty, and smelly. He raised his leg, as if to kick me out. Is there no limit to the humiliation you have to endure if "radish sprouts" grow on your legs?

"Pardon me." A young woman whom I had never seen before chimed in. She had a narrow jaw and was quite suntanned. Who is she? My shins may be green, but unfortunately,

I'm neither chartreuse nor a poet. The flash of a smile, like a
magician's card trick, jogged my memory. "I'll pay. I'm sorry
for the difficulty."

Perplexity and frustration on the face of the mustached
man, whose prey had slipped through his fingers.

The young woman removed her glasses from her purse
and put them on. White-rimmed glasses, round as the eyes of
a damselfly. Don't give me a shock! If it isn't the nurse from
the urology clinic! Again, the woman's spontaneous smile. My
face must have revealed the relief of recognition. The mustached man looked resigned.

"You saved me. I was wondering what would happen.
Surely you can explain . . . why I . . . this situation I'm involved
in . . . why in the world . . ."

"You need trousers, right? Do you know your size?"

"I'm sorry. I'll be sure to repay you."

"Don't make promises you can't keep. Up to ten thousand yen in aid is available to you. Those chino pants. He says
they're seventy-four hundred yen. Cheap, but they seem dur-
able. . . ."

"Excuse me . . . the catheter, is it still necessary?"

"What a pest you are! And what's that thing—hanging
from the IV hook?"

"Squid organs, I think."

"You must be kidding."

"The tube in my chest is still in too. . . ."

"Can't you take emergency measures by yourself?"

Again the flashing smile. Maybe it was a smoke screen
against the register clerk, who was eavesdropping. After paying

the bill, Damselfly led me to the rest room beside the staircase.

"This one's for women."

"Now is no time to be concerned with trifles. Sex differences and such are nonsense anyway."

Leaving the inner door open, Damselfly peeled off my blanket. The first thing she noticed were the thriving patches of "radish sprouts."

"I wonder if I can't wash them somewhere. They were soaked in sewer water."

"Why bother? Think of it as fertilizer."

"It's no joke. This is my precious food supply. You people threw me out without even a banana."

"So you like bananas?"

"Very funny."

Compactly tucked away in Damselfly's large bag was a complete emergency kit, as befitted a member of her profession. She grasped my penis between her experienced fingers, wrapped it in sterile cotton, quickly pulled out the tube, and dropped the end of it into the toilet. Urine spurted noisily out of the bag, swollen to the bursting point.

"If I'd gone on like that, I might have developed uremia."

"But you haven't, right?"

"How did you know that I'd come here?"

A drop of blood oozed from my penis. The nurse pressed the glans with sterile cotton, and though I didn't intend to, I quickly began having an erection.

"Silly!"

Damselfly gave my penis a rough flick with her fingertip. Her asparagus-like finger stung painfully. I quickly pulled on the new chino pants, then the canvas running shoes. When I folded the blanket and tucked it under my arm, my pants slipped down.

"I don't need this IV tube any longer either. If you cut the top and bottom off, it'll probably do for a while as a belt."

"Very strange." The nurse cocked her head as she examined the tube. "This isn't a tube; it's some kind of plastic cord. A super-strength fishing line? Anyway, there's no chance of your bleeding, so I'll cut it."

"To think how I suffered from this thing. . . ."

The nurse pulled out a pair of small scissors, and first cut it off about two inches from the collarbone. She carefully inspected the area of the skin where the tube had been held securely with bandages. She touched it and cocked her head again.

"I don't know about this. Have a specialist examine it soon. Right now it doesn't seem to be contagious."

"But it hurts."

She carelessly severed the squid organs, tossed them into the toilet bowl, and flushed the toilet. The angry organs bubbled and swelled. For a while they clogged up the hole, and the water began to overflow. Finally they disappeared, along with the loud gurgling noise.

"You could use this to protect yourself, couldn't you?"

Damselfly handed me the stainless-steel IV pole, then rushed out of the rest room. I followed right behind her, but she looked back and sighed deeply.

"Don't follow me!"

"But where should I go?"

"You have no choice but to return. It's not as if you have

anywhere else to go. . . ." She pointed down stiffly and said, "You know very well . . ."

"Yes, I know. But there's just one thing I'd like to ask: Do women really go for chartreuse men?"

There was no reply.

This time it was all downstairs, I had little to carry, and my movements were unrestricted, so it was far easier. At the second iron door, the graceful Baroque music died out, and I was enveloped in darkness. At the third iron door, the stench of sewage again assailed me.

The sound of water, slapping against the side of the boat, mingled with sighs. The introduction to Pink Floyd's latest hit. The boat that had been pursuing me, with the female squid organs hoisted high over the bow, wasn't waiting for me any longer. I crawled up onto the bed and closed my eyes.

The dry chino pants felt wonderful.

CHAPTER THREE
river of fire

The walls of the canal narrowed and changed to hand-hewn rock on which shovel marks were clearly visible. The current seems much swifter here.

The waterway made a right-angle turn. My field of vision expanded. A terrible stench. It's a tannin mist. My nasal membranes dilated. Then, the blinding flash of a strobe. A sparkling river beach appeared before my dazzled eyes.

Am I dead? Did I die and make my way to the netherworld? Sadness welled up in me. I rubbed the bridge of my nose, and a meaningless song verse escaped my lips.

Farakumba hanagumba merabenda
Rub it in red pepper oil
Wrap it in banana skin

The melody is "Night Deepens on Tannin Road." Tannin Road is a route for transporting tea that intersects with the Silk Road.

Sharakumba sharabunda saragenda

The stern jumped. The boat plunged headlong into a waterfall basin. I must be hallucinating. The canal I was drifting on was near the mouth of a river, at sea level. There can't be a waterfall basin lower than that.

Have I fallen to the bottom of the earth? Is this hell?

A rock scraped the bottom of the boat. Or else the bottom of the boat scraped a rock.

We ran aground.

The boat disintegrated and floated off. Only my bed was left standing on the riverbank. The sun shone through a canopy of clouds, and the cliffs were etched with wispy strokes of vermilion. Is it the lingering glow of sunset or the rosy sky of dawn? I seem to have lost all sense of time while I was meandering down the culvert.

The sky clouded over. The shimmering golden afterworld turned omelet-colored. Large and small crags and stones, the color of withered leaves, of carrots, of pumpkins . . . a lava plateau peppered with sulfur. So this must be the first section of hell. Isn't there a hot-spring souvenir called "lava candy"?

Something that looks just like pumice stone and crumbles easily between the tongue and the roof of the mouth.

A sulfurous gust whipped around the riverbank like a whirlwind.

Is this the river of the underworld?

I was lying on my stomach, so I used my knees as a fulcrum to lift my upper body and sit up. Because of the dense patches of "radish sprouts," I couldn't flex my knees freely. I rolled up my pants cuffs and sat cross-legged. "Radish sprouts" puffed out like a magician's handkerchiefs between my pants cuffs and shoes.

My vantage point rose by about two feet. When my field of vision expanded, the desolate landscape appeared even more ghastly. If I really have died, I must have crossed the boundary between life and death quite uneventfully.

"I've come to the conclusion—and this is an old-fashioned view—that in your condition, hot-spring therapy is the only hope. Preferably a sulfur spring, one that's as concentrated as possible."

"Like Hell Valley . . ."

"Exactly, like Hell Valley . . . assuming there's an inn willing to take you in . . . those legs of yours will certainly not make a good impression on the other guests. . . ." The doctor scribbled something on a tag, attached it to the bed leg, and shoved the bed with all his might out of the operating room.

"Don't take it personally. Dawn is coming, so do watch out for reckless drivers!"

Slowly the bed began to move. It was as if I'd willed it and, at the same time, as if it was beyond my control.

So is this where he sent me—the address on the wet, illegible tag?

When I peered down I could see the bottom of the river perfectly. Not only through still water, but even through gentle waves, everything looked crystal clear. For the lower reaches of a sludge waterway it seems far too clean. Does sulfur have such a purifying effect? It looks as though you could drop a line in and catch a rainbow trout. But threadworms are about all that can survive in a sulfur spring.

I took off my shoes and dipped in my toes. About one hundred degrees Fahrenheit, ideal for an open-air bath.

I submerged my feet up to my ankles. I kicked the water, alternating legs. The grime between my toes rinsed away, and immediately I felt refreshed, as if my entire body had been cleansed. It must be the purifying effect of the sulfur. I pulled my pants cuffs up higher and submerged my legs to midcalf. Maybe the "radish sprouts" polluted by the canal water will be sterilized and become edible again. My stomach throbbed with hunger.

I plucked one sprout from the root. It looked lovely. Perfectly white, juicy, pure. The double leaf at the tip, too, was deep green and fresh. Even the root branched out gracefully and showed no trace of debility. Maybe the notion that a sulfur spring kills parasites is a fable. Relax. A finicky beggar won't get much of a take. It's probably more naïve to expect bathing in hot springs to effect an instant cure, like a potent medicine.

I crushed the sprout between my fingers and sniffed. The odor of hard-boiled egg yolk mingled with the distinctive fresh fragrance of "radish sprouts." It was clearly different from the vile smell of methane or sewage.

Even so, I didn't feel brave enough to eat it right away. Bacteria can't be detected by merely looking and sniffing. You need a microscope and at least some basic knowledge of bacteriology. If I asked a health center to examine it, I'd probably have to wait at least three days. Even if the absence of bacteria were confirmed, the toxicity of sulfur would still be undetermined. Wait a minute. Isn't hydrogen sulfide mildly alkaline? I took a tiny lick with the tip of my tongue. It's salty. It tastes like sodium salt. They say it's salt water that preserves pickles. Maybe there's no need to worry. Besides, supposedly the water in hot springs is safe to drink, as long as you don't overdo it.

Now let's not be rash. At times like this, patience is of the essence. I should bathe repeatedly for at least half a day, then scrutinize the "radish sprouts" for any changes. After that will be soon enough to consider eating them. I can't claim to be starving at this point.

An even more chilling thought. Suppose in two or three days the treatment takes effect and the "radish sprouts" simply drop off like a moth-eaten fur coat. It could very well be a superficial recovery; the eggs of threadworms might be hatching in the pores. . . .

It's too unpleasant to imagine what would happen next. Shameless parasite though it is, there's no doubt that a plant is preferable to vermin. Threadworms might resemble vermicelli, but I wonder if you can eat them raw. "Radish sprouts" have actually eased my hunger any number of times. As long as I'm not fazed by other people's reactions, I must say they're an extremely convenient source of green vegetables. Without consulting an expert, I can't say whether my balance sheet shows a deficit or a credit, but surely the sprouts aren't a total liability. My partner absorbs liquid and lymph from my shins, and through photosynthesis produces carbohydrates. I eat those and convert them to energy. Assuming that energy is sufficient, then together we constitute a closed ecosystem. Come to think of it, the earth itself is a closed ecosystem, isn't it? If I think of myself as a miniature earth, what's there to grumble about?

Of course, if the "radish sprouts" continue their advance, forge across my knees, and head for my upper body, what good is being a closed ecological system? If my entire body becomes covered with vegetation, I'll have no choice but to find a job in a carnival freak show. Even my chances of that are probably slim. A monster isn't likely to attract much attention here in hell.

Suddenly the screen of clouds slid open. Evidently it's morning. A red filter appeared over the bank near my bed, and the irregular surfaces of the sulfur crystals stood out with dazzling clarity. Even my mood brightened. Time for a soak in the river.

I got up and took off my pants. My field of vision expanded more. Behind a cliff that was blocking a third of the view to the west, the top of a faded signboard became visible. What a relief! This place isn't deserted after all. Of course, since the sign is facing the other way, I can't tell what it says. If it says "Drinkable," I'm in luck. . . . I can rest assured both that the water is clean and that the sulfur isn't toxic. Then again, it might say the opposite: "Dangerous ✲ Keep Out ✲ Do

Not Drink the Water." But the instructions on the doctor's chart guided me to this reality; what can I do but meekly accept it? From the start, it's not as though I've been at the helm. I let the bed take the lead, and here's where I've landed.

I slid myself slowly into the river. After making sure there was no one watching me, I faced downstream and urinated for a long time. Peeing naturally, with no catheter, feels so good that I want to do it again and again. I waited for the bubbles to flow away, then walked around the bed. Volatile moisture, dry moisture . . . with each step, sulfur crystals crunched underfoot, trailing wispy streams of smoke.

Suddenly a warning came over a bullhorn.

"No bathing without a permit!"

It's close by. The volume is loud, but the voice isn't forceful. It's high-pitched. If it belongs to a male, his voice hasn't changed yet. Or is there a crack in the speaker's diaphragm? In either case, I'm surprised there's someone on duty so early in the morning. Depending on how you look at it, it could be a good sign. The fact that surveillance is necessary means there are illegal bathers here. It must be a very popular health spa with a steep bathing fee.

Let's mull this over a bit. I shouldn't be so quick to pooh-pooh the doctor's chart.

Someone darted out from behind the cliff as nimbly as a bug. Sure enough, it's a child. He was five or six, or possibly an underdeveloped seven- or eight-year-old. An old gray sleeveless undershirt that reached to his knees. Pointed chin, bony ribs, long, shaggy hair. From his left shoulder hung a money collector's bag, like a train conductor's, and under his left arm he clutched a bullhorn. His air of professional pride was pathetically touching.

"Do I need a permit? I came by water, so I don't know the procedure. Where's the manager's office? Afterwards I'll stop by and get permission."

"How about buying a coupon book right now?"

"Unfortunately, I don't have any money on me. I'll sign an IOU at the office. . . ."

"What's your occupation, mister?"

"What's yours, pal? You're a minor, right? Aren't you violating the Labor Standards Act?"

"I'm a child-demon. Your 'Labor Standards Act' and whatnot have nothing to do with me."

"A child-demon?"

"A little demon . . . a demon-boy."

"What is this place?"

"It's Hell Valley, as if you didn't know."

"What's the name of this river?"

"Sanzu—the river of the underworld."

"You mean I'm on the Riverbank of Sai?"

"And you pretend not to know. . . . Those funny grass boots you're wearing, are they shin guards?"

"I was referred by a clinic."

"Don't you mean by a funeral home?"

"Can you contact someone who knows what's going on?"

"What's the matter, don't you trust me?"

"My doctor prescribed this place; he said a sulfur spring would help."

"Then show me your prescription. If you have a prescription, your insurance will cover things. . . ."

"I left everything in the clothes basket at the clinic."

"Ooooh, that's bad. The rules here are strict."

There's no sense getting involved with this urchin. I picked up my shoes and pants from the bed and, ignoring him, I boldly began climbing up the bank. Probably on the other side I'll find a town with shops and restaurants and lounges for the resort guests. Who knows, if I'm lucky there might even be a treatment center connected with a university hospital here. What was that called again—physiotherapy?

The child-demon scooped up a small stone by his feet and threw it at me. For someone his size he pitched a fastball with a mean spin; the stone hit me squarely on my right upper shin. Luckily, thanks to the cushion created by the "radish sprouts," I didn't sustain any injury, but the pain shot all the way to the sole of my foot. My opponent is tougher than he appears.

"Hey, take it easy!"

"Get back in that bed right now!"

"I just wanted to have a look at that signboard. What does it say?"

"I'll read it to you, so do as I told you." He scampered as agilely as before and disappeared behind the cliff. Just then a temple bell tolled. It sounded like a small bell, but it had a clear, piercing tone.

"It's six o'clock. The 'Help Me! Club' will be here any minute. If you want a bathing pass, ask the club leader."

"Won't you read that to me?"

"Here goes."

The demon-boy began to chant, his voice flowing desolately through the bullhorn. The melody resembled a Buddhist pilgrim's hymn.

> *"This is the tale of the Riverbank of Sai—*
> *The lonely limbo for children's souls,*
> *Nestled beneath mountains in the netherworld.*
> *Just to hear it wrings the heart.*
> *Youngsters of two and three, four and five,*
> *Little ones, all under ten,*
> *Gather on the Riverbank of Sai.*
> *'How I miss you, Father! How I miss you, Mother!'*
> *The voices wailing these laments*
> *Are voices from another world*
> *Whose sadness pierces flesh and bone.*
> *The task these children must perform*
> *Is collecting stones on the riverbank*
> *And building memorial towers.*
> *'I set down the first stone for my father,*
> *I set down the second stone for my mother.*
> *I set down the third stone in memory of*
> *My brothers and sisters in my hometown.*
> *During the day I can play alone,*
> *But around the time when twilight nears,*
> *Suddenly a demon from Hell appears.'*
> *'What are you kids doing?' he growls.*
> *'The father and mother you left in the world*
> *Don't perform rites for your repose.*
> *From morning to night they only moan*
> *Of cruelty, grief, and misery.*
> *Your parents' laments are your punishment.*

Don't blame me!' The demon swings his iron club
And topples the children's little towers.
Just then the stones on the shore turn red;
The flowing river bursts into flames
That burn all creatures to the bone."

Silence.

He had chanted it in a singsong way, as if he'd just memorized it, so I didn't understand half of it. Probably the little demon himself didn't understand it very well. But one verse was lodged in my memory—"I set down the first stone for my father, I set down the second stone for my mother." I've heard that phrase before. I don't know where I've heard it, but it's engraved in my memory. A song that brims with a strange nostalgia, like a plaintive melody resounding in a bottomless well.

Already I couldn't look directly at the eastern sky, it was so radiantly bright. The ice sculptures on the Riverbank of Sai seemed undaunted by that dazzling brightness.

The child-demon continued.

"Right next to the song is a wind gauge, with 'WARNING!' written in big red letters, followed by an exclamation point. 'When the wind velocity is three or less, bathing is prohibited. Danger of gas poisoning. Long-term parking may damage your car engine. The management accepts no responsibility.'"

"What's the wind velocity right now?"

"Between five and six. You don't have to worry. It almost never gets to three or less. Once in a while on a calm evening."

A kind of marching song, chanted by an amateurish chorus of voices, drifted toward us on the west wind.

"Help me, help me, help me, please;
Please, please, won't you help me, please."

"What's that?"

"It's the chorus of the 'Help Me! Club.' I said so, didn't I? 'It's time, so they'll be here any minute.' "

"Help me, help me, help me, please;
Please, please, won't you help me, please."

"They're all children, aren't they?"

"They're all child-demons. . . . Well, mister, take care of yourself. The night shift is over now. . . ."

"Take me with you into town, will you? I want to make a phone call."

"I told you, if you need anything, you better ask the leader. He's in charge."

The "Help Me! March" was getting closer. I returned to my bed and put on my pants, so I wouldn't be reprimanded. Out of the corner of my eye, I noticed something appear at the far left side of the cliff. I looked up and saw six children, whose long, unkempt hair and baggy undershirts were identical to the first child-demon's. They were marching in step, military style, single file in order of height, separated by regular intervals.

"Help me, help me, help me, please;
Please, please, won't you help me, please."

The child-demon in the lead shouted an order.

"Left face; halt!"

They didn't seem very well trained. In a disorderly fashion, they faced left and formed a line, so that their backs were turned to me. Their disheveled hair tumbled down to their faded, size-L undershirts; they reminded me of mobile hand-carved anthropoids.

I wonder if there's a road on the other side of the bank.

An orange mini-van arrived, rattling noisily, like the lid on a boiling kettle. A dauntless-looking man in his thirties with close-cropped hair got out, his navy-blue synthetic jacket flapping. Apparently this is the leader. On his left arm was a blue armband with white writing, but unfortunately, from where I was I couldn't decipher it. The leader stood at the middle of the row, facing the child-demons, and quickly inspected them. When he noticed me, his hands dropped from his hips and remained at his sides. Confused and defensive.

"Good morning," shouted child-demon number one. "First action item: at present there is a suspicious character . . ."

The leader interrupted him and began questioning me directly. The entire row of child-demons turned around to look at me.

He pointed and moved his finger up and down. "From where, and how, did you bring it in here—that bed?"

"I didn't 'bring it in.' I drifted here on a fishing boat. The boat ran aground, broke up, and floated away. . . ."

"It's the truth. I saw it with my own eyes."

Child-demon number one's unexpected corroboration, or

else his self-defense. The leader silenced him with a gesture, as if shooing away a fly. "These facilities are under municipal management. The regulations must be strictly observed."

"Please phone and see. The doctor who examined me at the dermatology clinic sent me here along with the bed. I left my wallet with my insurance card and things in the clothes basket there. . . . Please do me a favor; if you can find out my credit card number, will you issue me a temporary bathing pass?"

"Sorry to pry, but the name of your disease . . .?"

"The doctor prescribed a sulfur spring."

"Circumstances aside, the view along the riverbank mustn't be spoiled. Article Three of the City Ordinances."

"Do you mean by me?"

"Of course not. That sort of bed doesn't belong on the Riverbank of Sai."

"Do you want me to move it? I can certainly try. In the beginning this bed used to move in response to my mental commands. I'll give it a try."

I knelt on the bed. The patches of "radish sprouts" were thicker than ever, so I couldn't bend my knees well. I summoned all my energy and sent a mental image of motion to the place between my eyebrows. The bed quivered. Scraping the riverbed, crushing the sulfur crystals, it slowly began moving forward. The child-demons along the riverbank cheered and clapped. But the little iron wheels weren't strong enough to ride over the loose stones; as the bed slipped from side to side, the wheels dug deeper and deeper into the gravel. The child-demons' rooting was futile, and my concentration began to flag.

"Go give him some help."

At their leader's urging, several child-demons came bounding down. They leaped from crag to crag, agile as water striders. They took hold of the bed, one on each side and four behind. As they began pushing it, they chanted:

"Help me, help me, help me, please."

But it's an ultra-heavy bed. Despite the assistance of the child-demons, it didn't have enough power to climb up the embankment. It was all it could do to move parallel to it.

"That's enough. Just move it downstream." The leader glanced at his watch and issued the order impatiently. "We'll leave it for now, as long as it doesn't spoil the scenery along the riverbank. After sunset, I'll send out a wrecker."

The child-demon on the left side of the bed murmured, "What's it like over there?"

It was a little girl's voice. The curve of her breasts was visible through her threadbare undershirt. When she brushed her long hair to the side, it looked as though she had deliberately smeared makeup over her face. Without that makeup, her face would probably be delicate and attractive. Remarkable sloping eyes. Wait a minute, I remember those eyes. The face peering through the window of the miniature train that we passed. Of course, I can't be sure.

"What do you mean, 'over there'?"

"City people."

The child-demon on the right shot her a meaningful glance. He kept winking and moving his forefinger around in a circle beside his head to indicate craziness.

A whistle blew. The leader began addressing the child-demons over his bullhorn.

"That's fine. Right around there. Everyone hurry and take your places. The first bus will be here any minute."

The child-demons scattered in all directions. They seemed to have assigned positions; without any hesitation, each settled into his or her own place. Some squatted down on relatively level pieces of ground, others behind rather large, flat rocks. The leader glanced around sharply, checking their positions. Then he descended the slope, calling out at the top of his lungs:

"Members of the 'Help Me! Club,' let's give it our best again today!"

"Help me, help me, help me, please."

The leader moved cautiously, as if testing the ground with each step. I realized that the footing was poorer and the slope steeper than I could tell by watching from below. I was impressed anew at the agility of the child-demons. The leader circled the cliff, crossed the river, and flopped against my bed in relief. He grinned wryly and said, "I'm getting old. I can't move like the youngsters anymore."

I could read the words on his armband now: "Tourist Division." He wore rubberized waterproof pants and high rubber fishing boots.

"Do you work for the city?"

"This is a really sturdy-looking bed you have. I've never seen one like it. Is it for foreigners?"

"It's made by the Atlas Company, which I gather is pretty well known for its hospital equipment."

"Anyway, you're a rare guest. A rare one indeed. I've never heard of a guest coming here by river, except for the corpses."

"This was what the doctor who examined me prescribed. Please phone him and see. I've forgotten the number, but I know the name and the place, so if you just phone Directory Assistance and ask . . ."

"Now, when it comes to corpses, usually four or five a year wash ashore here. According to the records, there was a year when the number exceeded thirty. But to arrive here alive is certainly rare. . . . Well, I suppose you haven't had breakfast yet, have you? Afterwards I'll be passing out sandwiches, so . . ."

"As a matter of fact, I'm famished, but I left my wallet in the clothes basket in the operating room. . . ."

"What's your academic background?"

"I did graduate from university. . . ."

"Leave everything to me. I'll think of something." The Tourist Division staffer climbed up and sat down chummily on my bed. He pulled a sheet from a packet of printed material in his pocket. "Here are the lyrics to the song you'll hear in the show that's about to begin. Use this to follow along. If you just listen, it's hard to understand. . . ."

"Thanks. . . . By the way, can I ask just one question?"

"You'll have to be quick about it. Do you hear that? It's the bus."

"Where does this river flow?"

"About a mile or so ahead is an entrance to a sulfur mine, but it's off limits. . . ."

"And beyond that?"

"It must be the ocean. Naturally, I've never been there."

"I came here by a canal that's almost at sea level. Something's odd. If you continued downstream from here, would you end up underground?"

"I guess there are rumors to that effect. . . . Look, it's here. We'll have to talk some other time."

A small bus arrived at the riverbank. Led by a female guide holding a flag, more than ten elderly people disembarked and lined up along the bank. The guide began speaking in a singsong way:

"Ladies and gentlemen, here we are at Japan's Number One Riverbank of Sai."

A golden dotted line sparkled in the row of people facing him. It must be the reflection from their gold teeth. "Japan's Number One" *is* a funny way to put it. These old folks have a sense of humor. The guide's explanation continued.

". . . The performance you are about to see is the tale of the Riverbank of Sai. As you all know, this is the tale of the pitiful children who dwell along the river that runs through limbo. Day after day they just keep piling up stones on the riverbank, with no chance of attaining Buddhahood. Among the one hundred and sixty-four places in Japan that boast a Riverbank of Sai, it is at this one alone that you can actually witness the stone-piling spectacle."

The gold dotted line disappeared, and the child-demons began to chant. It was a two-part chorus, of sorts.

"This is the tale of the Riverbank of Sai—
The lonely limbo for children's souls,
Nestled beneath mountains in the netherworld.

Just to hear it wrings the heart.
Youngsters of two and three, four and five,
Little ones all under ten,
Gather on the Riverbank of Sai.
'How I miss you, Father! How I miss you, Mother!'
The voices wailing these laments
Are voices from another world
Whose sadness pierces flesh and bone.
The task these children must perform
Is collecting stones on the riverbank
And building memorial towers."

He was right; seeing the words made it much easier to understand.

" *'I set down the first stone for my father,*
I set down the second stone for my mother.' "

All together, the child-demons began piling up stones.

" *'I set down the third stone in memory of*
My brothers and sisters in my hometown.
During the day I can play alone,
But around the time when twilight nears,' "

The child-demons threw themselves into piling up stones faster and faster. Whether because of differences in skill level, or the differences in shape of the stones scattered around the area, the height and size of the towers varied. Many of the old people began fingering their rosary beads out of a sense of foreboding.

> " 'Suddenly a demon from Hell appears.'
> 'What are you kids doing?' he growls."

A drone of sutra-chanting mingled with the rhythmical clicking of the rosary beads. Finally several old people were overcome; they sank down on the ground and wiped their noses with the backs of their hands. The child-demons rose to a half-standing position and worked ever more fervently.

> " 'The father and mother you left in the world
> Don't perform rites for your repose.
> From morning to night they only moan
> Of cruelty, grief, and misery.
> Your parents' laments are your punishment.' "

The sound of sutra-chanting swelled. Each child-demon tried to protect his tower by encircling it with his arms.

> " 'Don't blame me!' The demon swings his iron club
> And topples the children's little towers."

At once, all the towers tumbled down. The thin, high-pitched wails of the child-demons. The weeping of the elderly.

> "Just then the stones on the shore turn red;
> The flowing river bursts into flames
> That burn all creatures to the bone."

The child-demons dropped to the ground one after another, then lay motionless, in the fetal position. The moaning of the old people. The wind began to howl. Vapor appeared at the river's surface, rose, and blew away.

"Ladies and gentlemen, did you enjoy our performance of 'The Riverbank of Sai'?"

The guide gave a meaningless wave of her flag. A navy-blue triangular flag with a white mystic symbol. The old people struggling to rise from their stooping positions. The guide's nasal, singsong, unctuous way of speaking.

"T h e   r o l e s of the 'young children' in the heartrending performance that you have just seen were played by the members of the 'Help Me! Club' of the Municipal Spa Center Nursery School. The Nursery School is a self-supporting organization whose operation depends solely on our guests' donations. Please give generously so that our 'young children' can continue to keep this splendid art form alive."

The city worker began applauding wildly. He nudged me with his elbow, so I reluctantly began clapping too. The child-demons returned to life, bowed deeply, and joined in the applause. The old people followed suit and took up the beat.

> "Help me, help me, help me, please;
> Please, please, won't you help me, please."

All of a sudden, the child-demons charged at the tourists. They lifted the hems of their long undershirts to form kangaroo-like pouches and accosted the old folks.

"Help me, help me, help me, please;
Please, please, won't you help me, please."

"It's intimidating, to say the least."

"They probably can't run the nursery school on city funding alone."

The ratio of men to women in the group was two to eleven. Maybe the men looked more generous; each of them was hit up by several child-demons.

Finally they called it a day. The old people were patting the child-demons' heads, rubbing their cheeks and hugging them, when the guide blew her whistle and urged them to board the van. They lined up regretfully and returned to the vehicle. The child-demons waved to them as they left. Somehow it reminded me of an alley behind a nightclub at closing time. To the departing customers, the exchange of farewells marks the end of a rare festive occasion; to the women seeing them off, it's a depressingly familiar daily ritual.

The bus vanished into the distance. The child-demons surrounded one of their number and began emptying the contributions in their kangaroo pouches into her canvas money bag. The money collector was a half head taller than the others; she looked like the girl with the sloping eyes.

"Let's go," the city worker urged me. "The next bus is in two hours. At the cafeteria in the Center, I'm afraid you'll have to settle for the one item that's offered for breakfast, a sandwich. A professional nutritionist sets the menu."

He crossed the shallows and began climbing the cliff, choosing his footing much more nimbly than when he had come down. I could barely keep up with him.

79

Suddenly he turned around and said, "Pardon me for asking, but what's wrong with the cuffs of your pants? It looks like it's hard for you to walk. You don't have sores on your groin, do you?"

"What do you mean by that?"

"To put it bluntly, people with a venereal disease, especially gonorrhea, tend to develop groin sores."

"You have some nerve. . . ."

"No need to get huffy. It's no big deal for a man to contract gonorrhea. There are any number of effective antibiotics. . . ."

"Well, I don't have a venereal disease!"

"It's just that it's our policy to prohibit people with a venereal disease from bathing."

"I told you I don't have one."

"As a matter of course, you'll have to be examined by our regular physician. It's a city ordinance."

The child-demons waiting for us on the bank greeted us affectionately. The girl with the sloping eyes flung the sack bulging with donations to the leader.

"Wow, it's heavy. . . ."

The staff member tossed the sack into the trunk of the mini-van.

"Well, let's give it our best again today!"

The child-demons began marching in step. Every face was flushed with pride.

"Help me, help me, help me, please."

The leader tossed into the backseat a paper grocery bag and a bundle of what looked like dirty laundry; then he unlocked the door to the passenger seat. The stench of mold and body odor, like a container of flammable garbage. Beneath the hood, that kettle of water began boiling again.

Except for the sulfur and steam from the riverbank, it was a completely ordinary country road. Shops were scattered here and there along it. Between the road and a copse-covered hill in the background was a vegetable farm full of withered leaves.

"What sort of farm is that?"

"Peanuts. You know, goobers, monkey nuts."

We were soon out of sight of the river. That makes sense. Upstream is the canal that joins the underground tunnel. Still, the topography is mysterious.

"Where is the coast?"

"In this area the road doesn't run straight, so it's hard to explain. . . . There, you can see it now. Just beyond the woods at the village shrine. See that rather modern-looking building? That's the Municipal Spa Center."

We passed the procession of child-demons. The one at the head of the line gave us a little wave; it was the girl with the sloping eyes.

"You know the girl who collected the money, the one with the sloping eyes . . . ?"

"Yes?"

"Has she been at the nursery school here for a while?"

"Aha, you have good taste. An appealing child, isn't she? She's slightly retarded, and we're taking care of her. She's old enough to be in school. . . . But why?"

"Does she have a sister?"

"You're really taken with her, aren't you? We can't have any hanky-panky, you know."

"The idea! It's just that something about her bothers me."

Don't be absurd. A "cut on the shin" means a guilty conscience, but what I've got on my shin is no cut but a "radish sprout" patch. I'm hardly in a position to sow wild oats. It's too late for me to make mischief, even if I wanted to. Sloping eyes and slanting eyes are all the same to me; I'm about ready to be castrated. With these bleak thoughts, I bid farewell to the girl of my fantasies.

The Spa Center was set back from the main road about fifteen hundred feet. It was midway up the copse-covered hill. The large hall on the first floor was also occupied by a branch of the district office. The office was surrounded by several counters, partitioned off from each other. Except at the windows for proof of residence cards and personal seal registration, there was hardly anyone around.

"Downstairs is the Spa Research Center. I have to put away this morning's donations, then I'll catch up with you. At the bottom of that escalator is a lounge with vending machines and things."

The man in charge of the child-demons pressed two hundred-yen coins on me, then trotted off down the narrow aisle between two counters, swinging his canvas sack.

Freedom at last. If I felt like it, I could even make an escape. Unfortunately, I had no intention of escaping. I headed slowly for the escalator. I was careful about how I walked, so as not to attract attention. But deep in my heart I hoped I'd run into the girl with the sloping eyes. . . .

I stepped onto the escalator, and after descending about three steps, I noticed a boy standing with his feet planted apart at the bottom. It looks as though he means to ride up. He doesn't seem to be fooling around. He's quite a bit older than the other child-demons. Maybe a junior high school student. If he can't tell the difference between an ascending and a descending escalator, there must be something seriously wrong with him. Apparently the boy was having trouble understanding why he couldn't ride up. He put his foot on the bottom step and was pushed back. He wasn't discouraged; he put his foot on again. The distance between us was rapidly contracting.

"Get out of the way! It's dangerous!"

I waved my hand back and forth wildly, but he didn't react. Only a few more yards. Suddenly the youth turned and faced the other way. He finally seemed to understand that when riding an escalator you're supposed to face the direction in which the stairs are moving. But to grip the descending handrails firmly with both hands and step back onto a step while facing the opposite way is extremely difficult. Your upper and lower body will be moving in opposite directions, and you'll end up falling forward.

"Move! Get out of the way!"

It was too late. I put my arms around the boy and leaned on him. He lunged forward and fell down, and I fell on top of him. The boy wailed. Many footsteps rushing toward us. Deft hands cover me completely with a blanket. It's the same treatment that violent patients receive. A needle pierces my shoulder. It must be an injection of anesthetic. I immediately drift into a sweet languor.

The next thing I knew, I was on a bed again. This time it was a much narrower bed, like a stretcher. I was in the corner of some corridor. I didn't feel particularly restricted.

"You've regained consciousness. That's good." The leader of the child-demons was peering down at me. "It was a mild anesthetic, and we injected you with an antidote and a stimulant right away."

"Outrageous, wouldn't you say?"

"Sorry about that. You met up with the worst person. Fortunately, there were eyewitnesses, so we knew from the start that you weren't to blame."

"Did you find out the phone number of the clinic I first went to?"

"You have nothing to worry about. Our doctor certified that as far as diseases that violate city ordinances go, all your results were negative. . . . This was easier on you than being forced to undergo an exam for venereal disease, wasn't it?"

"Did he have an opinion about the condition that requires hot-spring therapy?"

"He didn't mention anything. I suppose he'd have to keep that confidential."

"I'd have liked to hear his advice about treatment, or at least his prognosis."

"He seemed to be totally baffled."

"Please let me meet with him—the doctor."

"That's impossible. The night shift is over and he went

back on the bus that just left. He was sent from the central hospital, and he only works nights. . . . However . . ."

"What is it?"

"He acted as if he didn't want to talk to you, even as if he wanted to avoid you."

"I might have known. . . ."

"But he approved your stay here, on certain conditions."

"Conditions?"

"Please don't take offense. First, that you don't use any indoor facilities. Second, that you bathe only at night, in the outdoor baths at the river, when there are no other guests around. Third, that you confine yourself to your bed. But since it may rain, for humanitarian reasons we're to provide you with a shelter that can tolerate extreme conditions."

I was kept waiting in the lobby for a while. I smoothed the creases out of a morning newspaper that someone had left and glanced over it, while keeping an eye on my surroundings. Evidently the world is falling apart. Regrettably, there wasn't a sign of anyone resembling a child-demon. Maybe the nursery school was in a different building.

The leader would drive me back to the Riverbank of Sai.

"Sorry to trouble you."

"I have to go there anyway. In another five or six minutes, the second busload will be arriving."

"Please don't forget to phone the clinic. It's a nuisance to be without my insurance card and my credit card."

"How about it? Have you any desire to work part-time for the 'Help Me! Club'? The instruction sheet for the lyrics of the river-of-the-underworld song that I gave you earlier has the correct pronunciation and interpretation. In return, we'll give you a free pass to the outdoor baths and three meal tickets a day. . . . What do you say?"

"Everyone does pretty well, don't they? Do they really need any more instruction . . . ?"

"The troupe does fine. But we're deluged with requests. Many religious groups are expanding these days, you know. . . . And the city is now considering the formation of a children's reserve corps. If possible, I'd like to create a two-shift system and lighten their burden, if only a little. . . ."

"Well, I'm not too confident, but I could give it a try. I can't do a thing until my cards come anyway."

I answered nonchalantly, but I felt a guilty thrill. If I end up living on the riverbank indefinitely, I'm guaranteed the pleasure of catching glimpses of that girl, if even at a distance.

He handed me a thin plastic box and a paper bag containing two canned drinks.

Clouds hung low in the sky, veiling the sun.

"It looks like rain."

"I hope your shelter comes on time. I'll try to expedite it."

My old friend, the Atlas bed. I lay down on the cool sheets. The natural resilience of the springs feels so good. First I opened the canned coffee drink. It's too sweet. I removed the rubber band from the little plastic box and opened out the napkin that was attached to the sandwich with a toothpick. The sandwich was a ham, egg, and vegetable combination. The wind howled. I took a bite of the sandwich and spat it out immediately. To my disgust, the vegetables were "radish sprouts." Even for a mean prank, it's too cruel. Nausea welled up in me.

I finally realized why that doctor had vomited so violently. It was right after he ate "radish sprouts" in fermented soybeans. Even if you don't mind the smell of your own dandruff, you can't stand the smell of someone else's. It must be the same physiological principle.

It started raining. It was more like droplets of fog than rain. In lieu of a shelter, I covered my head with the blanket, then I fastidiously picked out all the "radish sprouts" from the sandwich. I took a little bite and swallowed it. I vomited. I devoured the whole ham and egg sandwich and vomited all of that too. Drenched by the rain, I went on vomiting.

CHAPTER FOUR

dracula's daughter

Tattered clouds tangled in the sky as darker clouds pushed through them from below. The shower grew ever more intense. I strained my ears, but there was no sign of the child-demons' "Help Me! Chorus" approaching. Has the second "Riverbank of Sai Sightseeing Bus" been postponed?

The sopping-wet blanket. It doesn't do much good to wring it out. The tent I was promised probably won't be delivered until this afternoon at the earliest. My nasal membranes tingled, signaling an oncoming cold. Since I'm already wet anyway, why not take a plunge in the river? I have access to an open-air bath; I ought to take advantage of it. I can kill two birds with one stone: treat the "radish sprouts" and ward off the cold.

I bounced up and slid down from the bed. I bumped my tailbone on a pipe and grazed the skin. That's about right; even back in elementary school I was hopeless at the vault.

Churned up by the squall, the river water was completely murky. My feet felt their way cautiously along the river bottom. Five or six steps from shore, the water suddenly deepened. When I crouched down, it came up almost to my chin. The warmth gently pervaded me. From my lower vantage point, the landscape appeared entirely different. Yellow-green lumps of lava, glistening with moisture, supported a boundless, clear bag of rain. It's like a crude painting of hell scrawled on the walls of a remote mountain temple. The last morsel of sandwich that I was clenching dissolved between my fingers. What's there to regret? This veil of mist on the landscape is certainly not my tears; it's the rain that's constantly spattering my face.

Nocturnal incontinence . . . sudden flush of moist warmth. As long as I don't mind people seeing me like this, it's a blissfully liberating sensation.

The wind swept around, and the mist cleared momentarily. About three hundred yards upstream was a fairly high hill where the opening to a tunnel was visible. That must be the canal that tossed me out, along with the boat.

The downpour continued to intensify. Crackling sounds, flickering lights. A swarm of cicadas, frenziedly copulating.

Suddenly a layer of sludge rose and plugged up the entrance to the drainage canal. It swelled into a tar cork. As internal pressure mounted, the cork began inflating like bubble gum. Finally it popped off, and a gray flash flood gushed out. It was organic and spectacular, like a whale pissing. (Of course, I've never actually seen a whale pissing.)

I dashed back to my bed. I had no desire to be swept along on a urine flood. But I was quickly overtaken and engulfed by filthy liquid. I recalled the eyes of a seabird I had seen on TV; drenched in oil discharged from a grounded tanker and transformed into a black sugar-candy doll, it was shrieking helplessly. I clung desperately to the bed frame. Water pressure thrust up the bed. Afraid that I might be wrenched away, I wrapped my legs around a rail and managed to clamber up. For a moment, I thought I glimpsed a row of cylinders under the bed. Are those emergency oxygen tanks? I didn't have time to examine them. I wriggled along the mattress on my stomach. I stretched out both arms, imitated a gecko, and prepared to be assailed by a second big wave.

I was spared. I had expected the wave to roll over me. Instead I floated on it, like a boat. The bed's front end tilted up, and it began gliding along the surface of the water. Do the cylinders under the springs act as floats? Is this an amphibious bed? That's not just fabulous, it's downright absurd—or is it?

The bed continued to glide. A surfboard riding the waves.

Nausea welled up in me again. The area between my stomach and esophagus convulsed repeatedly. This time it seemed to be seasickness and not a reaction to the "radish sprouts" in the sandwich. Crashing against waves, shuddering, the bed whizzed along.

In a twinkling the Riverbank of Sai receded into the distance. I'll probably never return there, or even drop by. Farewell, child-demons. I feel a bit sad. Those figures in their size-L undershirts were endearing, despite their shabbiness. I'd like to hear the "Help Me! Chorus" just once more. And that sloping-eyed, slow-witted girl haunts me. I can't believe she's a complete stranger. She seems like a certain "someone" who's built a little cottage in a corner of my memory and has been dwelling there quietly for a long time.

The waterway narrowed and deepened.

Suddenly, disaster. A barricade marked "NO ENTRY" blocking my way.

This must be the site of the sulfur mine that the city worker warned me about. The barricade was just a makeshift thing put together with wires and wooden planks, but it stretched across the river, and a collision seemed inevitable. Considering the weight and speed of the bed, we'll probably crash through it. I don't want to be injured. I huddled down and covered myself with the blanket.

There was nothing like a crash. There was less resistance than if the barricade had been a picture drawn on wet paper.

Again we rushed into a dark tunnel. It wasn't half as high as the drainage canal where I'd taken refuge after leaving the Daikoku Department Store. If I sat up straight, my head would bump the roof.

After a while there was a real collision. From the back of my head to the nape of my neck came the sound of frozen meat cracking.

I don't know whether I finally regained consciousness or I simply woke up.

A nearly perfect full moon, close to the horizon. The color of a well-used copper pot. It must be evening again. That means over half a day has passed since I lost consciousness. It's cold. I tried turning my head. Besides the pain, a disturbing sound of bones grating. The creaking of a corridor in a deserted wooden school building.

Struggling to cope with the pain, I slowly observed my surroundings. Something is strange. I'm not in my bed. This place is soft, but it isn't flat. There are soccer balls lying around. A cool, watery kitchen smell. Surely it can't be a pig slaughterhouse with just heads rolling around. They're like purple cabbages. In the moonlight, does green look purple? No, these days shredded purple cabbage is often served with pork cutlets, as a garnish. It must be a fad.

I tried rubbing the surface of a slightly deformed ball. It tore and peeled off. When I rubbed it again, another leaf rose to the surface. A third . . . a fourth . . . They were becoming more and more crisp and resilient. I folded one in half and sniffed it. My vomiting reflex was stimulated. It smelled like "radish sprouts." The sweet, tangy scent of a vegetable that can be eaten raw. I was becoming convinced that I was in a cabbage field.

I was anxious about the vegetables on my legs. I rolled up the cuffs of my slightly damp trousers and gently stroked them. Even though they had been exposed to moisture, they lacked vitality. Many that my fingers touched fell out with no resistance. I want to examine in the light the pores from which sprouts fell out. If the plants have begun withering at the roots, thanks to the sulfur spring, I'll be overjoyed. . . . But if new plants are sprouting in the pores . . . The area was itchy, but I forced myself not to scratch it.

Where on earth has my bed gone? These damp pants and shirt feel terrible. I'd better get back in bed naked.

I raised my upper body. My lower back didn't hurt as much as my neck. In the darkness I could make out some kind of structure. It appeared to be fifteen to thirty feet away. The moonlight was behind me, so I wasn't sure, but if I imagined it to be a bed, it looked rather like one. A canvas awning was stretched over it, like the rain shelter you see on roadside stands. Maybe the shelter I was promised has been delivered. At the foot of the thing appeared to be a heap of bedding. I pricked up my ears, expecting to hear signs of human activity. Only silence reverberated. Or is it the whoosh of a train? The distinctive sound of iron wheels chafing against rails. It also sounds like the wind howling at the ocean. The frictional sound of winds of different velocities.

The bedding seemed to move. I must be imagining things. I should go back. They say a dog is drawn back to its house by the scent of its body there. I've begun to feel a nostalgia like homesickness for my bed. After all, I've been living in it for quite a while now. Besides, the humidity in this cabbage field is awfully unhealthy. My dank underwear feels like it's becoming a hotbed for microbes.

I took a step, then stood still.

It's no illusion. The bedding is moving. Awkwardly, clumsily, but it's definitely making its way toward the pillow. Who could it be? A vagabond? Can I charge him with illegal entry? Or unauthorized borrowing? Or theft?

The bedding crouched over the control panel on the headboard and began operating the switches and dials in ear-

nest. The mechanism was so complicated that I had given up
on operating them almost from the start. There was even a
warning on the plastic plate: "Patient: Do not touch." Besides,
the bed wasn't connected to an electric source. Even if you
could operate the dials correctly, nothing would happen. If the
creature doesn't have that much sense, maybe it isn't human
but an anthropoid.

But there was a response. The lamp in the awning flickered a few times, then came on. It's that fluorescent light whose
sources are concealed. It's glaring. Two sprinklers on each side
of the lamp. It doesn't seem as though an awning would need
sprinklers; maybe they're part of a preassembled roof. Naturally, the bed is equipped with a battery that's stored with the
oxygen cylinders below. If a power outage occurs during surgery, it can be dealt with. This bed is even more fantastic than
I imagined.

That moving blanket can't possibly be an ordinary vagrant;
the thing knows too much. Who can it be? Maybe the lawful
owner, who can claim possession more convincingly than I.
Maybe I'm the one who'll be charged with a crime. I don't
have the deed of sale for the bed, nor do I have any proof of
residence.

The intruder was covered from head to toe with the blanket. The material had a large green-and-brown check design;
depending on how it was worn, it could look flashy or drab.
Now it looked drab. The blanket was cast aside and the rear
view of an old woman appeared. She placed her bottom between the arches of her feet and let her upper body sink into
her pelvis; the movement reminded me of a stack of freshly

pounded rice cakes slowly settling. The dark-blue kimono, tinged with the color of withered leaves, the baggy material, the sash that was the hue of well-aged yellow pickles . . . She picked up something by her knees. If it isn't a shamisen! It suits her so well it's embarrassing. I'm no expert, but it looks like the slender-necked type. She plucked a string with her pick and began tuning the instrument. The sight was so pitiful that I couldn't bear to look straight at her.

"That's my bed. Get away from it!"

The old woman turned around. She had no eyes. Not only no eyeballs, but no traces of eye sockets. Wrinkles covered her entire face, from brow to chin. She's ghastly.

"Don't be so cruel; listen."

Again the feeble strumming of strings. It was mostly noise.

"Enough! I don't want to listen to that sort of thing!" I pulled up a head of cabbage and pelted her with it. "Clear out of here right now. If you don't . . ."

"Thankless child!"

Her wrinkled throat undulated like a frog's. Gruesome!

" 'Child,' you say?"

"You don't recognize your own mother? You're a disgrace."

"She's been dead for years."

"Look who's talking. You've just crossed the river of the underworld yourself."

"You mean I'm a dead man?"

Her pick slid across the strings, producing a hideous rising twang.

"Crimson camellia,
Floating on the surface of
Shinobazu Pond."

"I said stop it!"

"Perchance it is
A spray of blood
Spurting forth."

"You're a fraud. I never heard my mother play the shamisen."

"Once you're in the other world, your tastes change. Especially if you have an unfilial son. Everything changes quickly. You don't even remember my face, do you?"

"That face of yours isn't even human in the first place. It's like an eyeless lizard or a dried-out worm."

"My eyes? I hated to do it, but I sold them. Of course, I got paid for them while I was still alive. . . ."

Suddenly the old woman let out a shriek. She assumed a squarely defensive posture and brandished the pick in her right hand. "Don't come any closer! Get away from me!"

She doesn't seem to be admonishing me. After all, I haven't budged. Even if she begs me to, I have no intention of getting close to her.

In my ear, a sweet voice that I'd heard before.

"Don't oppose me. Let me handle everything."

A nurse in a short skirt was standing beside me, whispering in my ear. Her breath had a slight scent. The very subtle fragrance of her body. She's the nurse who's so good at drawing blood. The one who rescued me from the guard in the Worldly Desires shop and took out the catheter. She's the nurse who wears the round glasses.

"How did you know I was here? You keep popping up unexpectedly. . . ."

"We'll talk later. . . ."

"That old woman seems really scared of you."

"Because it's the hour for drawing blood."

"It's incredible. How does she know if she can't see?"

"Probably by hearing."

She licked her lips and removed from the black leather case under her arm a large, 20-cc hypodermic syringe. She flicked it lightly with her finger. It's the same finger that flicked my stiffening penis in the bathroom of the Worldly Desires shop.

"I won't let you!" screamed the old woman.

"Now be a good girl, Granny. Let me have a little blood."

She switched the hypodermic needle to her right hand, straddled a furrow in the cabbage patch, and began approaching the old woman on tiptoe.

"Don't come near me! Get away!"

She certainly does have keen ears. She thrust out her chin, raised herself up on one knee, and readied her pick. From the tip of the pick came a metallic gleam. I wonder if it conceals a blade.

With the bed as a stage, an eerie confrontation began. The old woman, enforcing her defensive stance by shaking her pick in a way that reminded me of leaves fluttering down from a ginkgo tree; Damselfly, her torso swaying rapidly on her long, caramel-colored legs, watching for an opportunity to inject the needle. I can't imagine that she'll be able to draw blood like that, although she'll probably succeed in intimidating her elderly opponent. Compared to the old woman's desperate attempts to ward her off, Damselfly's movements exude "sexual" confidence. The decrepit navy-blue kimono versus the well-starched short white skirt—there's no contest.

"Don't come close; get away from me!"

"You realize, don't you—tonight's the full moon."

"It's all the same to me; I'm blind."

"Just a tiny bit; even one cc will be enough."

"Blood, indeed." The old woman's voice broke, and she blew her nose hysterically. Probably since she had no eyes, her tears came out of her nose. "How could I have even a drop of the stuff?"

"Let me check to see whether you have or you haven't. Don't you know that I've been voted 'Miss Blood Collector' for three years straight?"

"I don't know anything about it."

"When it comes to wielding a needle, I'm sure of myself." Damselfly prepared the syringe and edged closer to her. "Even the 'Dracula's Daughter' Medal is within my reach. I'm determined to draw another twenty-two hundred and six cc's by the end of this month."

The nurse's left hand shot out, quick as a minnow, but the old woman's pick parried it as nimbly as a snake. She kept running her fingers around her mouth, as if to remove her false teeth. Something is coming back to me. It's a memory from early childhood. The old woman wiped the false teeth that she had removed with the ball of her thumb, and in a wink she slipped them inside her collar. Still, she hadn't been able to hide the gold crowns on her upper and lower canine teeth. (They say this is the way they tell the corpse of one Japanese from another in foreign airports.) This may indeed be my real mother.

"It's werewolves, not Dracula, that come out on the night of a full moon." Maybe because she had removed her dentures, my mother's corpse was constantly smacking its tongue, as if it were sucking on a lozenge. "I know that much; I often watched those movies on late-night television."

"And you can't even see."

"Better watch your step, sonny. If you drive me away, this vampire lady intends to suck you dry."

"Quit calling me 'sonny.' "

"Why?"

"It makes me sick."

"Is that so . . . ," murmured Damselfly earnestly. "On the night of a full moon, a 'werewolf' *is* much more appropriate. You know, maybe you're a werewolf. When you're treated like a boy, it hurts your feelings."

"A wolf?"

"How about climbing up here and letting her stroke those bushy shanks of yours."

"Nothing doing. Anyway, it's just ordinary grass."

"You have grass growing on your legs?" the old woman asked in a pesky voice, her curiosity aroused.

Taking advantage of her momentary distraction, the nurse plunged the needle into Mother's carotid artery. The old woman's pick instantly brushed it aside, and blood oozed from the back of the nurse's hand.

"Damn it!"

The vampire lady growled and licked the blood from her hand. Then she snatched the shamisen from the old woman's knee and brandished it in the air.

"Have pity on me!"

Mother cringed and prostrated herself. She held her head between her hands and implored. She sounded as though she were sucking on candy because she had removed her false teeth. She doesn't seem to be putting on an act. Is she afraid that she'll be struck, or is she worried that her shamisen will be smashed? Her terror and pleading seem genuine. Her shoulders are writhing in anguish too.

Suddenly I was overcome by pity and tenderness. My tear ducts tingled. I don't especially dislike my mother. But I don't like her either. Old people are all revolting. As I silently apologized to my mother, I became captivated by the vampire woman's short skirt and began having an erection. If she took off her glasses, what sort of eyes would she have? Her plain glasses created a strong reflection so I could hardly see her eyes. They may well be gorgeous sloping eyes.

"In that case, hurry and leave!"

"Give back my shamisen and I'll get down right away."

"Be quick about it."

Damselfly tossed her the shamisen. There was no reverberation, just the sound of the wooden frame warping.

"We'll probably never meet again, so I have one last favor to ask—please."

"Nothing complicated."

"That scene where I scolded the boy for being unfilial—let me do that once more. It won't take even three minutes. Please, it gave me so much pleasure. How I wanted to recite those lines, even once, while he was alive."

"If that's all she wants, why not humor her?" Damselfly urged me. I relaxed and exhaled. I was confused by her sudden change in attitude.

"I forget. Which scene was it?"

"He's going to let me do it! Hooray!" She put in her dentures and brought her shamisen into playing position. "First, Mother will strum the shamisen. Then, sonny, you'll start complaining."

"I told you to cut that out—'Mother' and 'sonny.' . . ."

"What should I say?"

"Didn't I use to call you 'Mama'?"

" 'Mama'!? Isn't that far more revolting?"

For the first time, the two women laughed in unison.

"Just don't use any nicknames or second-person pronouns and it'll probably be all right."

"Fine with me." She brought the pick to the strings. "All right, now let me have it!"

"How?"

"Like before, don't you remember? About the bed."

The harsh twang of the strings.

"I can't remember."

"Anything will do."

"Even so . . ."

The sound of the pick striking the instrument's body instead of the strings.

"Crimson camellia
Floating on the surface of
Shinobazu Pond."

"Cut that out! It gives me the creeps."

"Perchance it is
A spray of blood
Spurting forth."

"Do that somewhere else!"
She nodded and skipped a beat.
"Thankless child!"
The two women breathed in unison.
"Are you satisfied?"
Damselfly flicked the syringe and smiled.
"How I wanted to say that while I was alive."
"I think I understand. Separating from a child is more crucial than separating from a parent. For kangaroos there's apparently no such thing as 'filial' or 'unfilial.' "
"What's that about kangaroos?" I impulsively demanded, but I was ignored. I wasn't expecting an answer anyway.
"I'm sorry to have troubled you."
Mother lifted herself up, using her shamisen as a cane.
"Yes, before dawn breaks . . ."
"Dawn? That's right, the moon is sinking. For some reason, when I wake up it's always morning."
No one answered me. The moon looked like a freshly

minted hundred-yen coin. Its lower edge, toasted over an open flame, had begun to melt. If that's west over there, the ocean must be in the leeward direction.

"I don't really resent you for being unfilial. . . . Well, take care of yourself. . . ."

Mother slid down from the far side of the bed. Again she removed her false teeth, slipped them into a pouch inside her collar, and inhaled the wind through her puckered mouth.

"You better wrap yourself up in the blanket. You'll be chilled by the morning dew."

The vampire woman lent her a hand with nurse-like solicitude.

"Thank you."

Mother faced the moon and began walking straight in its direction. She's like a nocturnal insect.

"How about keeping her company part of the way? Don't worry about me."

You don't have to worry about me either. Fortunately, Mother didn't seem eager for my company. She set off more surefootedly than I'd expected. She seemed to have already forgotten all about me. My chest ached. It's true; living in another person's memory is more stressful than you might think.

"I w o n d e r w h e r e she intends to go."

"She probably doesn't even know herself. Instead of standing there, why don't you come up here?"

At last. The words I've been waiting so long to hear.

"I'm hungry—starving."

"But just let me draw some blood, okay?"

"When you're hungry, your blood sugar level drops, right? When their blood sugar drops, men's sexual desire is stimulated, but with women I hear it's the opposite."

I folded the damp blanket, hung it over the rail at the foot of the bed, and quickly scrambled up onto the mattress.

"Lie down."

"While you're at it, will you check the 'radish sprouts' on my shins? These chino pants you kindly bought me have gotten all dirty; can I take them off?"

I didn't have an erection yet. Probably, between the memory of being flicked and my unrealistic expectations, my autonomic nerves were too tense.

"When I was alone, I wasn't that conscious of it, but an outdoor bed is a strange thing."

I took off my pants and lay down. She wrapped an elastic band around my upper right arm. To tell the truth, I was more concerned about the condition of my shins. To bare my soul even further, I of course wanted the situation to develop to where I could let myself have an erection.

"Pardon me," she whispered. While she sterilized the area with the alcohol swab, Damselfly's knee touched my side. The split-second sensation of needle puncturing skin. Her pride was justified; there was almost no pain and no superfluous movement.

"What you said about the 'Dracula's Daughter' Medal— is that true?"

"Of course not. But it's a charming fantasy, isn't it? If you think so, why be crass and try to root out the facts?"

Right now I want to deal with this thirst and hunger. But is there a restaurant open at this hour? Not likely. It isn't that sort of locale.

The moon tumbled down with a thud. Dawned tinged the eastern sky the color of mint. As the vampire woman put away her hypodermic equipment, her knee continued to rest against my side. Her knee and my side are both naked. The only barrier to our genitalia is a mental one. Besides, this bed isn't all that wide. Under the circumstances, it wouldn't be a bit unnatural to advance to the next stage.

"How are the 'radish sprouts' doing?"

"They don't seem as moist as before."

"Do you still find them revolting?"

"For the time being, a sexual relationship is out of the question."

"Why? I don't think I'm contagious."

A clamor of children's voices drifted toward us on the wind. Is it the child-demons on the Riverbank of Sai?

"A group of students going to school. Sickening. I'm no good with children. They have no self-control."

Five or six children with flashlights in hand were approaching us at a distressing clip. They were about a hundred feet to the west; they walked in single file, probably because it was a country road. One of them must have noticed the bed. It would be odd not to notice it. If you're surrounded by cabbage fields as far as the eye can see and suddenly a parade float pops into sight, your curiosity is naturally aroused and you want to have a closer look at it.

The children changed direction and began marching

straight toward the bed. They surrounded it and gawked uninhibitedly.

"Get lost. I'm not on display."

"Go ahead and do it. You were just about to, weren't you?"

"Do what?"

"You know."

A boy in a student uniform cap, apparently the oldest, made a fist and poked his thumb between his forefinger and middle finger in a vulgar gesture. He glanced expressionlessly around his companions. Four boys and two girls. Everyone was waiting silently, with bated breath.

"Nitwit!" In a flash, Damselfly grabbed the child's hand, pulled him toward her, and whipped out a hypodermic syringe.

"This is a bloodmobile. Do you know your blood type? I'll bet you're type A."

"Leave me alone!"

The child shook her hand away and scampered off. But he didn't go far. The circle of children surrounding the bed just widened a bit.

"Don't mind us, get on with it!" Student Cap repeated mechanically. His deadpan manner must have been due to extreme tension. When that occurred to me, I noticed that the whole group was panting heavily, like a wind blowing in through a half-open bus window.

My stiffening penis had shriveled.

"Do you know of a restaurant in this area that's open?"

"Aren't you going to do it?"

"We've just finished."

Tension turned to relief and rippled through about half the group of children.

"There's a noodle shop." A little girl pointed into the darkness.

"Where is it?"

"Go out onto the expressway and it's on the first corner. That road's a shortcut for long-distance trucks."

We found the noodle shop right away.

Most of the customers were truck drivers, most of them seemed short on sleep, and the only sound that broke the silence was the slurping of noodles. We looked like a happy couple, so we immediately became the center of attention.

"I see you in a new light, I really do. The look on that kid's face when you said 'We've just finished' was priceless. . . . We'll chuckle about that for some time to come."

Unfortunately, I wasn't able to stay cheerful for long. The Roast Pork Healthy Special that we ordered included miso soup that was garnished plentifully with "radish sprouts."

proposal for a new traffic system

Naturally, I couldn't bring myself to touch the miso soup with the "radish sprouts." I left half the pork and noodle soup, but I managed to polish it off. To leave part of a dish and to polish it off sounds like a contradiction. But that's actually what happened. I set a goal, drew a line with my chopsticks, and gobbled up the portion that I'd marked off, so in a sense, I both left some and polished it off.

Damselfly took care of the bill; it was tacitly understood that she would. She had to know that I'd left my wallet in the clothes basket at the clinic. It was a short-term loan until I got the wallet back.

"I prefer curry rice for lunch."

"Was it that bad?"

Outside the sliding door was a monochrome morning. It was the hour when a range of shade intensities are discernible but it is still too early for objects to have taken on any color. The first train had already left, and evidently there was still some time before the second one's departure. Traffic was scarce on the road in front of the station. A warm breeze was about to banish the dawn. It would probably be another hot day.

"Shall we go back to the bed for the time being?"

"I suppose so; there's nowhere else to go. . . ."

"The more I think about things, the more puzzled I am. Take my mother, for instance. How the devil did she ferret out the whereabouts of my bed?"

"Do you know what a dog whistle is?"

"I've heard of it."

"It's a whistle that makes a high-frequency sound that isn't audible to humans. I guess it's used in training. Not only dogs but bats and other creatures can utter ultrasonic sounds. I wonder if, amazingly enough, your mother has become attuned to ultrasonic waves in compensation for her loss of sight. The way she brandished her pick, as if she were fencing, made it seem as if she could see her opponent."

"And are you in charge of blowing the dog whistle?"

"Don't try to bait me."

"When it comes to mysterious behavior, you're second to none. You always come to my rescue in the nick of time. You're like the defender of justice in the comic books. All that's missing are the red cape and the theme song."

"Just a series of coincidences. For example, my happening to come by here this morning . . ."

Her words were cut off. Snip went a sharp scissors. We had just begun walking along the expressway. Low, red-tinged roofs and, behind them, a vast expanse of cabbage fields. Damselfly alerted me by nudging me in the side with her elbow. She had spotted it in the east. Beneath a row of ginkgo trees, their leaves gleaming in the sunlight, a flat iron object was approaching, grazing the curb. Incredibly enough, it looks just like my bed. Yes, it definitely *is* my bed. Its awning-like roof was gone; it must have been shaken off or been stolen. Since it had no tires or springs, it vibrated rapidly, like a baby buggy. It waddled up to us as if it could barely support its own weight. A cockroach bulging with banquet leftovers . . . No, it has four legs, so it's more like a turtle.

"It's obviously terribly fond of you." Damselfly cocked her head sarcastically and looked up at me. Probably because of the angle there was no reflection, and I could finally see through the lenses of her glasses. Sure enough, she has sloping eyes. Eyes that look as though they're constantly apologizing for something. She's the third one since my journey on the bed began. First, there was the little girl on the amusement park train that I passed in the underground tunnel; next, the re-tarded child-demon on the Riverbank of Sai; and now, Damselfly, the self-styled Miss Blood Collector. Something ran through the series of encounters that resonated in me like an echo. Were the similarities coincidental? Or were the three encounters related?

"Anyway, it's moving by remote control. But who's the controller, I wonder?"

"It's chirping . . . it sounds like a sparrow or a grasshopper."

"The wheels are digging into the sand."

A middle-aged jogger rushed past us from behind. Probably a midlevel manager; his waistline was like a barrel. He stopped and looked at the bed. He crouched down and peered beneath it. Maybe he wanted to see if it had an engine. He apparently lost interest immediately. He shaded his eyes with his hand and glanced up at the sky. It looked like it was about to rain. Then, as if nothing were out of the ordinary, he turned around and trotted off, his pedometer rhythmically ticking away.

"Let's you and I ditch it too."

"Why?"

"It's embarrassing, isn't it? It would be different if it were a dog or a cat."

I strode off defiantly, and Damselfly reluctantly quickened her pace. But it was naïve of me to think that we could simply give it the slip. Although the damn thing had been as poky as a child's tricycle before, it suddenly picked up speed and began following us at a set distance. The screeching of its wheels intensified. The shrillness of that sound resembled a shrike more than a sparrow. It was a bizarre spectacle—a man and a woman fleeing, pursued by a bed.

"We'll attract even more attention this way. Since it was kind enough to come and offer you a ride, how about showing your gratitude by getting on it?"

Damselfly took my elbow. Graceful fingers, like those of a model in a commercial for laundry detergent. I must have been hexed; my feet were rooted to the spot. The bed pulled up alongside us and quietly halted. Damselfly took a nurse's uniform cap from her shoulder bag, pinned it on her head, and reversed her green belt with an orange flower pattern to its white side. She was instantly transformed into a nurse. Absolute authority. I gave in and scrambled up, shoulders first, spun my body halfway around, and lay down on my back.

We were directly under a pedestrian bridge. It's a bridge between two bus stops that's used for crossing to a train station. The station is made of wood and has a nostalgic peaked roof. Its name is written in garish crimson letters. It's a well-known place name. You don't need to check it on a map. A name that carries a specific meaning in familiar figures of speech and proverbs. But I'm in no rush to divulge it. After making sure that I won't cause trouble for anyone will be soon enough.

A gull passed under the bridge, and three crows flew after it. The scent of the ocean was in the air.

Damselfly deftly smoothed the wrinkles out of the sheets, shook out the damp blanket, and spread it over me. When I surrender totally to her, I go falling down and down into a hole; it's a deliciously regressive sensation, like returning to infancy. I've never taken a sand bath, but I imagine it's a similar feeling. The erectile nerves in my penis are preparing for action. Have I turned into a sex fiend?

"Aren't you going to get on?"

"Are you serious? We could be charged with public indecency."

She stood by the side of the bed, just placed her hand lightly on the rail, and the bed meekly obeyed. If I were to look carefully, I would immediately notice something unnatural about her posture. She's not using the muscles in her legs or hips at all. The bed is propelling itself. But her nurse's uniform is skillfully camouflaging that unnaturalness. She seems to be escorting a critically ill person. The patient's condition is far more serious than if he were riding in an ambulance. His death march brims with such pathos that it is agony to witness. Anyone would avert his eyes.

I noticed someone at the handrail of the pedestrian bridge. He was leaning forward, resting a rather large television camera on the rail and observing us through a wide zoom lens.

"Wait. Someone seems to be spying on us from the bridge with a camera."

"Don't look. Pretend you don't notice."

"He's a real beanpole. He doesn't look Japanese."

"I told you not to look, didn't I? He's been hanging around me."

"Why don't you give him the brush-off?"

"He doesn't seem like a bad guy. And his Japanese is really good."

"So he *is* a foreigner."

"He says he's American."

"Have you reported him to the police?"

"Of course not. He's renting an upstairs room at our house."

"Is your house around here?"

"It's just after the next signal. The first corner on the right after crossing the railroad tracks."

"I wonder if this darn bed was intending from the start to go to your house."

"Maybe so. There's a carport for deliveries that we're not using now. . . ."

"Is this your day off at the clinic?"

"I quit that job some time ago. Didn't you know?"

"Some time ago?"

"Shall we be going? It's about time for the first bus to arrive. . . ." Damselfly tapped the edge of the mattress as if she were prodding a horse, and again the bed began to move forward.

"Because since Mother died, there's no one else to mind the shop."

"What shop?"

"Tobacco and cosmetics. The American tenant has put up various other signs too. . . ."

"What kind?"

"For instance, one advertising a local chapter of the 'Japanese Association for Death with Dignity,' and . . ."

"He's a shady character. He's still taking pictures, you know."

"I told you not to look."

"Why?"

"He says a person who isn't conscious of the camera looks more natural."

"Are you in on this? It sounds like you two are on pretty intimate terms."

"His limbs are long and slender, like a spider crab's. The other day, in some department store's newspaper advertisement, there was a photograph of a famous sculptor. Who was that? It's slipped my mind just now. Anyway, he looks just like that sculptor's figures. He's my type. It's a shame he's so hairy, though."

"Hairy? Where is he hairy?"

"Except for his face and palms, everywhere."

"Then he's no different from an ape."

"It beats 'radish sprouts,' doesn't it?"

For a while our march continued in silence. It kept time with the erratic rhythm of the wheels.

> Farakumba meragumba sharabenda
> Rub it with red pepper oil
> Wrap it in banana skin

"About what time was that?"

"What?"

"When your mother died."

"We held the seventh-day memorial service just last week."

"That's strange. Wasn't it the day before yesterday that I dropped by your clinic?"

"Apparently you ought to have your head examined too."

"If it means looking at that picture of the pig without a tail, no thanks. From the start you people have treated me like an imbecile. It's infuriating."

"Can you remember? From that point, where and how you wandered around?"

"Do I need to explain?"

"Not really, but . . ."

"Well, I'll be glad to. Actually, the story is quite simple.

First I was dumped into some underground shaft at a construction site by a tow truck that hauls off illegally parked cars. After a while the bed began running on rails. . . . Say, do you have a younger sister?"

"I had two, but one died, and I guess the other one ran away from home."

"Just as I suspected. Before coming here I met two girls with terrific sloping eyes. One, as I was riding through that tunnel, waved her hand at me from the window of an empty train that passed us going in the other direction."

"How dare you? Calling attention to a woman's physical defect . . ."

"What do you mean, 'physical defect'? I thought the girl was really attractive. . . . I mean it. . . . In that empty train, all alone . . . I can't get her out of my mind."

"Do you know what my nickname in high school was?"

"What?"

"Dumpling."

"Because you were sweet?"

"No, because my eyes droop; 'down in the dumps,' you know."

"I love sloping eyes. They make me want to lick the corners of them."

"Go on with your story."

"At the end of the tunnel was a boat dock. A squid-fishing boat came to pick me up. There was a huge, covered sewage ditch—if it were a road, it would be the width of four lanes. It must have been a canal at one time. It's been turned into a culvert. After drifting down that for a while, we arrived at the basement of the Daikoku Department Store. There we were attacked by another squid-fishing boat. In a flash, I escaped into the Worldly Desires shop. . . . Just as I was about to be charged with shoplifting, you appeared, like a rescuing goddess. Do you mean to say that was a coincidence? Your next appearance was this morning, in the cabbage field, where I was fighting with my mother. Just before the confrontation turned bloody, suddenly, with exquisite timing, you intervened. . . . It was too perfect. You know something that I don't know. Am I right?"

"I never miss my morning walk. Have to keep in shape, or I'll lose my knack for drawing blood."

A bell rang intermittently; three times. The second train must be pulling up to the platform.

"As soon as I get my wallet back, I'll repay you for what I borrowed at the Worldly Desires shop and for that pork and noodle soup we just had. . . . I left it in the clothes basket at the clinic."

"Go on with your story."

"Okay, after the Daikoku store, huh? I went back to the squid boat. Where else did I have to go? After a while the boat was tossed out of the sewage canal, and it ran aground. I found myself stranded on the Riverbank of Sai. It was dawn then too. So that's how I figure that the second day began this morning."

"The Riverbank of Sai is the entrance to the river of the underworld, isn't it? Don't hundreds of aborted fetuses gather there and chant as they pile up stones?"

"There's an outdoor bath at a potent sulfur spring—I think it did me a bit of good. Maybe it's my imagination, but the 'radish sprouts' on my shins seem to be wilting. . . ."

" 'I set down the first stone for my father'—Isn't that how
it goes?"

"I memorized the whole thing. I had a part-time job
teaching the lyrics. They gave me a free bathing pass and meal
tickets. . . .

"This is the tale of the Riverbank of Sai—
The lonely limbo for children's souls,
Nestled beneath mountains in the netherworld.
Just to hear it wrings the heart.
Youngsters of two and three, four and five,
Little ones, all under ten,
Gather on the Riverbank of Sai.
'How I miss you, Father! How I miss you, Mother!'
The voices wailing these laments
Are voices from another world
Whose sadness pierces flesh and bone.

"After that comes the famous 'I set down the first stone
for my father' part . . ."

" 'I set down the second stone for my mother . . .' "

"Do you know who they set down the third stone for?"

"No."

"See? Almost no one knows. But there's no one who
doesn't know about 'the first stone' and 'the second stone.' Shall
I tell you who the third stone is for?"

"You really are an oddball. Your tastes are too austere for
a man your age."

"It's not really a matter of taste."

"But you become lively when you chant that old hymn."

"You don't understand. There are at most only about ten real child-demons. And the chant is just part of a performance put on by the children at the nursery school run by the Municipal Spa Center. They give the show for the tourists who come there on sightseeing buses, and they collect donations from them. One of those child-demons is a girl with sloping eyes who looks a lot like you. Did I already tell you this? She wears a size-L sleeveless undershirt that comes below her knees; it looks really good on her too. . . . They say she's an orphan. . . . I wonder how she'll survive from now on. The chorus has quite a good reputation, and apparently they're able to operate the nursery school just through contributions. . . . There's something about that melody that's deeply moving to a Japanese. It's written in the classical 5-7-5 prosody . . . like this: 'See, the signal's green. Look again before you cross. This way, then that way . . .' "

"You really *do* like it."

"How could I 'like' that eerie incantation? If I liked that sort of thing I wouldn't have fought with my mother at this late date. I admit that I'm unfilial, but to make amends, I don't mind setting down a stone or two for her."

"It was painful for me to watch; I just lost my own mother, you know. . . ."

"I know what you mean. Watching a figure like that vanish into the distance is harmful to your mental health. . . . Shit, if only she hadn't played that shamisen."

"It's wretched, isn't it? Being lonely even after you're dead. . . ."

"If I ever have a chance to meet her again, I might feel like shedding a few tears for her. . . . How about you? Has your mother's spirit already appeared to you?"

"In my case, fortunately or not, there's no chance of that. Look, do you see that? Right over there. The flower arrangement just beside the railroad tracks."

The road curved sharply to the right, and a narrow, two-lane road without a sidewalk forked off to the left. There was some kind of signal, but there was no railroad crossing gate. It was a sharp corner; the intersection formed an acute angle of less than thirty degrees. Lodged in that sharp angle, a wedge-shaped two-story building. A sign saying TOBACCO in red letters on a white background. Has the sign been there since the National Tobacco and Salt Corporation provided official signboards? At the point of that wedge, a bouquet of flowers. White and purple flowers, like the balls on the tips of toy fireworks.

"Did she die there?"

"She died in a traffic accident. Our American tenant recorded it in detail for us. Smashed to smithereens. Like mincemeat. He captured the whole thing on video, so if you'd like to see it, I can show you. Having that film made it easy to negotiate with the insurance company. . . . So she can't become a ghost. If she does appear, she'll look like hamburger or meatballs."

I didn't know whether to laugh or not. The joke glinted and vanished, like a deadly fishing lure.

"It does seem like a place where there'd be a lot of accidents."

"I wonder if the American living upstairs chose our home

to board in because of his graduate degree thesis. He says the frequency of accidents around here, relative to the amount of traffic, is the highest in Japan. Furthermore, the mortality rate is tops in the world. It's the subject of his documentary film, *Fatal Accidents*."

"Is that sort of record of any value?"

As the bed approached the railroad crossing, from the direction of the station came a warning whistle, probably signaling a train's depature. The green traffic light went on. The tune of the children's nursery rhyme "Time to Cross" began playing briskly, as if to hurry people along. Still, it's an unusual kind of signal. Inside a large rectangle, the word RUN is flashing. Does it literally mean we should run? The bed stood firm, like an ornery mule.

"That signal is urging us to hurry, isn't it?"

Damselfly shook her head slightly and just gazed across the tracks in the direction of the station. She didn't budge either.

A warning whistle. Blood swirled around my eardrums. A three-car train, apparently used for short distances, passed, rending the air. The intermittent warning whistle. Modern, orange cars.

About ten seconds after it passed, the RUN sign stopped flashing.

"That's a strange signal. It seems intended to *cause* accidents."

"Do you think so?"

"Don't you suppose your own mother was tricked by that signal?"

"But she was slightly color-blind, and she couldn't read English at all. . . . It's possible that she rushed out on purpose. . . ."

"Suicide?"

"She was an unlucky person. My sisters and I inherited our sloping eyes from her. We all came from the same field but different seeds. None of the fathers stuck with her. I'm 'Dumpling,' so that's not so bad, but my mother was called 'Sad Sack Keiko' by the people in our neighborhood. It wasn't just that her sloping eyes made her look sad; she was really a sad person."

"But I like those eyes. I like all three of you."

The bed began moving slowly. It entered the railroad crossing, and when it came to the rails it suddenly picked up speed and jumped over them. Those grooves must be hazardous for the small wheels. Didn't I hear that once somewhere a primary school student got her heel stuck in the gap between the rails and died?

"The carport is in back, around the corner. . . ."

Damselfly spoke to the bed as if it were a trained watchdog. The bed slowly circled around the unpaved street. Behind the wedge-shaped building was a space just wide enough for the bed to squeeze in.

"Can you let me stay here for a while?"

"If you've made up your mind . . ."

Plastered all over the sliding glass door were various fliers and signs the likes of which I had never seen before. They're visible from the railroad tracks, but do these signs have any effect as advertisements?

NEW TRAFFIC SYSTEM
RESEARCH CENTER
(PROPOSAL FOR POPULATION CONTROL
THROUGH TRAFFIC SIGNALS)

INTERNATIONAL
DRACULA ASSOCIATION,
JAPANESE BRANCH OFFICE
(NOTE: SUICIDE BY PEOPLE OVER 65 YEARS
OLD—APPROXIMATELY TWICE THE NUMBER OF
TRAFFIC ACCIDENT DEATHS—6,300 PEOPLE)

WOLFSBANE AND MORE —
EVERY TYPE OF POISONOUS PLANT AVAILABLE

JAPANESE ASSOCIATION FOR
DEATH WITH DIGNITY—
FOR DETAILS, PHONE 03-3818-6563

JAPANESE EUTHANASIA CLUB —
ORGANIZATIONAL MEETING

KYOKUNEN KARATE SCHOOL
CHIROPRACTIC CLINIC—
MASTER HAMMER KILLER

"Any way you look at it," I said, "that sort of sign seems highly suspicious."

"The green RUN sign?"

"You ought to take it up with the authorities."

"I hear it's under investigation. But unless you know who and where the authorities responsible for it are, you can't do anything about it. There's an awful lot of red tape. Of course, I know perfectly well who's responsible for it, but why should I tell you?"

"Does that American have a philosophy?"

"Don't you have a philosophy?"

"I have a bit of interest in kangaroos, but when it comes to having a philosophy . . ."

"Shall I make some tea?"

"Won't the American be coming back anytime now?"

"He can drink canned coffee."

"In any case, my throat is really parched."

"No farther than the entryway!"

"I know!"

I got down from the bed. She offered her shoulder. Small, delicate joints inside the rather meager flesh. I walked around a lush fig tree and went through the wooden back door. The door was made of one thin cedar board, and there seemed to be a trick to opening it. A concentrated, sour-sweet blend. The odors of the entryway, the woman, and the young American. The scents of vegetable stew, tatami, and mildew.

At her prompting, I sat down on an old animal skin that had been spread over the threshold.

"What sort of fur is this?"

"It's a souvenir from the American. He says it's a kind of kangaroo."

"I wonder if he isn't Australian, rather than American."

"You know, I feel kind of sorry for you."

"Why? No, never mind. I understand."

"I think you're a really good person. . . . Ordinarily, when I'm with a man of your age, I become more lively, but for some reason, it doesn't happen with you. I just don't feel excited. . . ."

"Because of the 'radish sprouts,' maybe?"

"That's one thing."

"It's all right. One of these days I'll go back to the Riverbank of Sai to live and look after your little sister."

The warning signal whipped through the house. The building shook and the floor vibrated. A train must be approaching the station. The crossing signal played the melody:

Time to cross
Time to cross

Damselfly suddenly froze, the teapot in her hand tilted midway toward a teacup. She looked as if she was waiting for something.

Nothing happened. The sound of brakes, barely audible, perhaps due to the direction of the wind. The train seemed to have stopped at the platform.

Damselfly brought the teacup toward the spout of the pot and pursed her lips.

"It's strange. I seem to be waiting for an accident. I don't just 'seem' to be; I really *am* waiting. Maybe it's become a habit, under his influence."

Outside the tobacco shop, a 50-cc motorcycle came to a stop. A large man, about six and a half feet tall, with video equipment hanging from both shoulders, dismounted from the toy-like saddle. Damselfly dashed to open the sliding door. The man was hunched over; the hair on his head was sparse. He looked boyish, but he had the chest span of a rhinoceros. If his body is hairy to boot, he must have abnormally high male hormone levels.

The American pulled out a microphone and panted excitedly.

"News, news, incredible news."

He acknowledged me, and with the help of gestures and facial expressions, he carried on three or four conversations with me at once. "A little while ago you let me film you from the bridge, so we already have a relationship." "Let's all be friends, okay?" "I'm in a hurry now, so let's save the small talk for later. . . ."

Damselfly hastened to conduct the introductions.

"May I present MISTER HAMMER KILLER."

She sounded as if she were announcing a pro wrestler. When I laughed, Killer laughed too. He tilted his body sideways and mounted the narrow, steep staircase, chortling all the way.

From upstairs, in a voice that demonstrated his powerful lung capacity, he declared in fluent Japanese, "I received word. They said a group of thirteen bikes is on its way."

Damselfly explained. "We have a contract with three other shops; we receive information from them. The Rolling

Bike Gang has a hangout on a mountain road above here.
We're planning a wholesale massacre. . . ."

"You're surprisingly bloodthirsty, aren't you, despite those
sloping eyes."

"I wonder if I've been infected." She took down a stainless-
steel container from a shelf and inspected her elastic band and
hypodermic syringe for drawing blood. "I don't understand it
myself. I'm really very timid, and I can't even stand to watch
other people fight, but drawing blood from people on the verge
of death doesn't bother me a bit. I wonder if I'm abnormal?
Maybe it's an occupational hazard."

The roar of the engine of a small two-wheeled vehicle
grew louder and louder.

"They're here! But isn't it too early?" Killer shouted from
the second floor. "They should have stalled them another
twenty seconds with the red lamp at the gasoline stand."

The whole group passed, beating wildly on drums made
from stuffed elephants. The warning-signal tune pealed out
belatedly.

Time to cross
Time to cross

After a few seconds the alarm whistle, then the ear-
splitting whoosh of a train.

Killer came down the stairs, beads of sweat standing out
on the pink flesh of his brow.

"What a pity," I remarked.

"Why?"

"I just felt like saying that."

"Hey, I'm easy. 'Research means waiting,' as they say."
He called to Damselfly, "Will you give me a can of iced coffee?
You're the one who's pathetic, huh? Since quitting the clinic,
your blood intake has plummeted. You'll have to come up with
a plan. . . ."

He sat down on the floor by the wall. His arms and legs
protruded beyond my frame of vision. What's that Earth Spider
Tribe, in Japanese legend? Reddish hair on the back of the
hand clenching the aluminum can. He seems just as Damselfly
described him. But I haven't an ounce of sympathy to spare on
him. My wound is much deeper than his.

"Of course, 'Killer' is a stage name or a pen name, isn't
it?"

"Right you are. It's my professional name. I only use it
for karate matches. You know how Japanese shy away from
using second-person pronouns. But they feel comfortable calling me by my professional name."

"What do you mean by your 'research'?"

"Are you by chance considering euthanasia?"

"Certainly not."

"No need to get nervous. But if you're ever so inclined,
I'll be glad to lend a hand. To put it plainly, euthanasia is the
perfect, totally pain-free form of suicide."

"I understand your research topic is 'Accidental Death.' "

"That's right." Killer smiled. His eyes drooped slightly and
he looked positively ecstatic. "In short, 'Accidental Death' is
the supreme symbolic expression of contemporary death. 'Accidental Death' is obviously suicide, and at the same time, it is
obviously murder. The assailant and the victim are intimates.

To delay death by hastening death is to balance the bankbook that we call 'civilization.' "

"Killer, do you intend to cohabit with this woman?"

"She's a nurse, so she doesn't need any sex education. . . . I didn't know what else to do, so I went out and bought *The Narrow Gate*, thinking I'd study up a bit."

"Gide's novel?"

"Novel? I thought it was a 'how to' book on seducing virgins."

"Disgusting." Damselfly took off her uniform cap and said in a low voice, "Americans aren't a bit ashamed of their ignorance."

"At least we don't play 'Barbie doll,' like a lot of middle-aged Japanese guys."

"Don't Americans read Gide's novels?"

"Do Japanese?"

"I've never read one," admitted Damselfly. "A book I read recently that I really enjoyed is *Hometown of the Wolf-Mouthed Woman and the Human-Faced Fish*."

"That story about Hanako the School Ghost is amusing too."

"What's that one about?"

"In the doo-doo toilet at a certain elementary school—actually, if it's the girl's lavatory, there's no distinction—when you knock on the door of the fourth stall and ask, 'Is Hanako there?' someone answers, 'It's me!' "

"That's a good one! Do you mind if I make some notes?"

Killer whipped out an electronic memo pad and began typing away. He was a young man after my own heart.

"Killer, what you said about Gide's book was a joke, wasn't it?"

"Japanese people are essentially kindhearted, aren't they."

Some mail slid through the mail slot. Damselfly flipped each letter into the wastebasket as if she were performing a card trick.

"Killer, in light of your philosophy, what's your view on kangaroos?"

"Are marsupials, in point of fact, free from morphosis or are they constrained by morphosis? That's a tough one, for sure. . . ."

Damselfly flicked the last piece of junk mail with her fingertip.

"No luck. It didn't come today either. Nothing but bills for membership dues; I can't trust the Dracula Society anymore."

"But they gave you that medal, didn't they?"

"You can find that sort of thing in a toy shop."

"They say that since the Ceaușescu regime collapsed in Romania, the postal system there has gone to pot too. On top of that, rumor has it that Count Dracula the Eighth has assembled a group of guerrilla fighters and is trying to take over Transylvania. . . ."

I drifted into a long nap. When I came to, I found myself back in my bed. There was curry rice in a food warmer by my pillow. I drank some hot milk and a can of vegetable juice. The tomato-and-green-pepper combination was pretty tasty. Tears sprang to my eyes from sheer satisfaction.

I dozed off again.

I woke up trying to wrap the blanket around my naked belly. It was pitch-dark, and I had no idea what time it was. The soles of my feet had been devoured by mosquitoes. I plucked a "radish sprout" from my leg, crushed it, and sniffed it. I didn't notice any change. I wonder what Mr. Killer and Damselfly are doing on the other side of this wall.

I pricked up my ears. All kinds of sounds are absorbed by the wind, so all kinds of sounds were brought to me by the wind. I pressed my ear to the wall beside me. The wailing of the wind was amplified, so suspicious sounds seemed all the more suspicious.

My neck began to hurt. I dozed off and woke up again and again.

It was probably near dawn when I gave a big yawn. My jaw creaked. I must have dislocated the joint.

I tried to move it back by myself, but the pain made me wince. If I just stayed still, the pain wasn't unbearable, but I couldn't stop drooling, and my hard palate was gradually drying out, so it became impossible to even talk.

I remembered a sign on the glass door.

**KYOKUNEN KARATE SCHOOL
CHIROPRACTIC CLINIC—**
MASTER HAMMER KILLER

Lost to all sense of discretion, I banged away on the door.

For a while a flashlight flickered, then the overhead light came on. It was Damselfly by herself, wearing a pair of thin crepe pajamas. No one had an alibi.

"What's the matter?"

Do I need to explain? It ought to be obvious at a glance. All I have to do is point back and forth a few times between my jaw and the sign on the glass door.

Killer staggered down, wearing only a thin bathrobe over his naked body, attire that sensationally exaggerated his physique. The smell of cheap whiskey?

The kangaroo skin was spread across the entryway, and I was forced to lie face down on it. I rested my jaw on Master Killer's knee. Long hair tickled my nose, and I began sneezing. With a shout, he delivered an elbow chop to the back of my head. It felt as though the bones in my ears were being extracted with pliers. I've never experienced such a violent medical treatment.

W h e n I r e g a i n e d consciousness I was in a different hospital. It seemed to be quite a large hospital. There were eight other people in the room with me. At the head of my bed hung a tag that read "Floor 8A—Orthopedic Surgery—Mild Case." The bed was somewhat narrower than the Atlas bed.

A strangely soothing sound. Inside the ice pack wrapped around my jaw, ice cubes are gently clicking together.

the wind's plainchant

Sleep infiltrated by sounds from the television, fragments of memories.

A long needle injects local anesthetic behind my ear and on the back right side of my throat.

My face is pressed against a glass plate, and some X rays are taken.

A large rubber hammer deals several sharp raps to the area around my temples. Thanks to the anesthetic, there is no pain.

Massage . . . a wet compress and an ice pack . . .

"A slight case of tendinitis, no damage to the bone. You didn't need to be hospitalized."

"But I lost consciousness."

"A temporary concussion."

A g a i n I l a p s e into sleep, again I dream.

The aroma of pork dumplings, a spray of curses. I can't grasp the meaning. My nose is tweaked. Tongues cluck. My face is slapped back and forth. The ice pack on my jaw is shifted to my mouth, a gag.

Some of it must have really happened. When I woke up, I had a slight nosebleed, and my cheek was hot and swollen.

I have no idea why I'm being subjected to such treatment; maybe it's a kind of torture, rather than punishment.

Suddenly a cicada sloughs off its skin. Or is it a snake's skin? No, it feels like a thicker garment coming off. More like a shell being shed by a lobster or crab. All at once the anesthetic sheath drops off and I become lighter. Apparently I've been under general anesthesia as well as local. Swaddled in a soft skin of moist nostalgia . . . Only my vision becomes razor-sharp and my eyes overflow with indescribable images. Rapture? Then, slowly, revulsion brought on by a creeping sensation. Fish eggs laid over the entire surface of my body.

I wiped my runny nose with the palm of my hand and saw that sure enough, my nose was bleeding.

What time is it? Probably either morning or afternoon.

White vinyl curtains on both sides of me. Partitions for ensuring a degree of privacy. Suddenly the curtain at the corner of the foot of the bed opened, and a pair of rubber-soled shoes entered without a word of warning. That's only natural. On a hospital ward, nurses aren't obliged to ask permission. A patient is merely a defective piece of merchandise that can maintain its human form only by being cast in a mold called a bed.

"Does it hurt?"

"Uh-uh," I whimpered softly, shaking my head slightly from side to side. Whether a nurse prefers self-restrained patients or clingy ones probably depends on her personality. In any case, during Round One I should just observe my opponent's moves.

"Here's the thermometer. . . . Let's change the ice pack on your jaw."

"The wind is really howling."

"Wind?" She seemed a bit sassy, maybe because of her peanut-like snub nose. "That's the sound of the air conditioner on the roof; it's starting to go out of whack. . . ."

"Not that sound, but throughout the sky . . . It's as if hundreds of harmonicas were scattered all over and people were blowing on them with all their might. . . ."

"That's a pretty fancy way of putting it."

"Because I can play a reed pipe . . ."

"Doesn't it hurt to chatter so much?"

"Talking doesn't seem to bother me, but for some reason, my nose won't stop bleeding."

The nurse glanced over the bedside chart, removed the thermometer and read it, then cocked her head.

"It looks as though you weren't injured badly enough to be hospitalized."

"But I was knocked unconscious, wasn't I?"

"If the oral surgeon gives permission on his rounds tomorrow, you're probably well enough to go home."

"As long as there are no aftereffects from the concussion. . . ."

"What a peevish patient! Since the orthopedist ordered it,
I'll change your ice pack for you, but that's all. . . ."

She adeptly changed the ice pack. My vision blurs again.
I gradually become aware of the fluorescent lamps across the
ceiling that provide a kind of indirect lighting, the sprinkler
wearing the glasses just like my father's, or my father's image
engraved on the sprinkler. The effects of the anesthetic return,
rolling through me in waves. Time seems to be streaming back-
ward, swelling the banks of sensation. Not quite euphoria, but
a soft, buoyant feeling.

"It *is* wind, after all. . . ."

"I can't stand blabby patients."

The nurse flicked my crotch through the blanket. Three
times in a row. Does she have a grudge against men?

Rubber Soles vanished as silently as she had entered. After a moment, the bed curtain on my left side fluttered. A back
scratcher was thrust in. Not one of those bamboo ones sold as
souvenirs at hot springs, but a wooden one, painted black, that
looked like a miniature totem pole. A souvenir from the
Philippines?

"I'm coming in, okay?"

A soft, husky voice. It's a bother, but I probably ought to
treat patients with greater seniority as cordially as possible. Besides, there are countless things I don't know about this hospital. I have to cultivate potential sources of information.

"Come in, come in."

The back scratcher drew the curtain, and a man of around
forty, his face as flat as a pancake, was sitting cross-legged on

his bed. A dauntless little man. The most striking thing about him was the dense growth of black hair on his shins, visible through his slightly open hospital gown. He kept tapping a cigarette filter against the back of his hand, blinking his eyes, and flicking his tongue over his upper lip as rapidly as a reptile.

"How could it be an air conditioner? It's wind, just as you say. I've been here nearly a half month, and this is the first time I've heard this howling sound. But it's pointless to defy the nurses. If they gave in to patients too easily, it'd injure their soldierly pride."

"Can you hear children singing somewhere?"

"Children?"

> " 'Help me, help me, help me, please;
> Please, please, won't you help me, please.' "

"That's creepy; it must be your imagination."

"Could it be an announcement at the train station?"

"On this windward side there's no train station. It's an illusion. If you strain your ears, you start hearing every sound that you imagine. They call it the north wind blown down by the mountain gods."

Behind the man was a window covered by white blinds. Pitch-blackness filled the cracks between the slats of the blinds. It must be night.

"About what time is it now?"

"Nine-thirty."

"Damn, I missed dinner."

"Rotten luck." He rubbed his stubbly face and laughed

evasively. Maybe this guy swiped my dinner. "They say Coca-Cola is the best canned drink for killing hunger pangs."

"What time is breakfast?"

"Do you have any dough? With dough, there's always a way. 'The devil himself can be bribed,' as the saying goes."

Hairy Shins seems to be staring at the area around my pajama pocket. I just realized that these pajamas are new. Damselfly's thoughtfulness? Or are they a present from Master Killer, in apology for the rough treatment that went awry? Whichever one it was, they were looking out for me. You can't even be admitted to a hospital without making a prepayment.

I casually felt around in my pocket. I seemed to have some thousand-yen bills. There must have been about ten of them. I gently pulled one out and looked at it. Sure enough, a thousand-yen bill.

"You *do* have some. Great; let me have it. But wait until lights-out at ten o'clock. What's your pleasure? Carp-shaped jam cakes? Or moon-shaped jam buns?"

"They're almost the same, aren't they?"

"They're totally different. I strongly recommend the carp cakes."

"Why?"

"They're crammed with bean jam to the tip of the tail. The bakers are conscientious."

"Either is fine. . . ."

Something fluttered in the evening sky. Probably some bats had been knocked down. I blew my nose. Blood oozed out.

"Will you let me have two thousand yen in advance?"

"Two thousand yen?"

"It's the going rate. A thousand yen for a box of twelve. The delivery charge is a thousand yen. That guy takes care of the sales tax. And it's nervy of me, but I get two sweets as a referral fee."

"Never mind. I'll go buy them myself."

"It's not so simple. There are patients who fill their faces and fly the coop, and besides, the hospital has a morphine stash. Hospitals are like jails when it comes to getting in and out of them at night. But luckily, there's an escape artist among us with three criminal convictions. He's discovered entrances and exits that even the security guards don't know about. He'll run errands outside for you, but the location of the passageway is top secret. I'll introduce you to him after lights-out; he's tight-lipped, a good guy. A thousand yen is reasonable, eh?"

My nose was running. When I wiped it on my pajama sleeve, some blood oozed out.

"My nose won't stop bleeding."

"There's something I want to ask you. . . ." He narrowed his eyes and tossed his mangled cigarette into the garbage. "Do you remember? I'm the one who slapped your face back and forth."

"So I wasn't dreaming after all."

"I tried to go easy on you. No hard feelings, okay? Your snoring was terrible. If I hadn't done it, a rougher guy might have really worked you over. Everyone's on edge because of this wind."

I stroked my face. It was still swollen and sore.

"Then I guess I ought to express my appreciation." I folded two thousand-yen bills into quarters and tossed them onto his bed.

"Save the sarcasm." He took out a fresh cigarette. "Get a load of these hairy legs. My ancestors were probably Jōmon tribesmen. Those hairy foreigners of the Neolithic era who're even mentioned in *Manyōshū* poetry. They were settled in Japan way before the Yamato tribe; I'm from a distinguished lineage."

I began to feel extremely uneasy. If he asked me about my shin hair, how would I respond? I decided to make the first move.

"I'm going to the toilet."

I sat down on the toilet lid, rolled up a pajama cuff, and looked. Nastier than I expected. If she saw this, even Hanako the School Ghost would probably let out a shriek and flee. It doesn't look like either leg hair or plant life; it's like a vegetable field abandoned after a flood. Feeble new sprouts among the nearly lifeless stumps. The whole patch will probably be rotten before long. I wonder what the doctor wrote on my chart. As soon as he realized that my jaw wasn't fractured, maybe nothing else mattered to him. Come to think of it, the nurse on rounds didn't pay attention to anything besides the ice pack.

When I returned to my bed, Neolithic Man was back in his bed, spreading out cards between his knees. I wonder if he's playing solitaire or something.

"If you see any you like, I'll give you a good deal."

They were not playing cards but pornographic pictures. A man and woman entwined. The fact that the faces were cut off made the photos seem totally amateurish, and all the more obscene.

"Polaroid photos, huh?"

"Yep. I took them myself. Don't be shocked—the girl is

my own daughter. Like daughter, like father, I say! But the guy
with her isn't me. I wouldn't go that far. . . ."

The wind knocked down two or three more bats. Someone's shrill moaning voice.

"What's that?"

Neolithic Man was getting impatient. "Hurry and decide;
I can't leave these spread out forever. I'll charge you five hundred yen apiece."

In my imagination I attached a face with sloping eyes to
the headless girl in the various photos, as if she were a paper
doll. Which photo does it go best with? There were three
strong contenders, but I was in no position to waste that much
money. I reluctantly chose one and quickly slipped it into my
pocket.

"Do you have change?"

"You can pay me later. Say, you have good taste. . . ."

"Does your daughter have sloping eyes?"

Thunder boomed in the distance. It sounds like a mountain exploding. As if incited by the noise, that moaning intensified. Neolithic Man gathered up the photos and tucked them
in his bellyband. Then he faced diagonally across the aisle, toward where the moaning was coming, and snarled, "Shut up!"

It had no effect whatsoever. In fact, the moaning grew
louder and louder. The person's chest seemed to be congested
with phlegm. First there was a long wheeze, and afterwards a
gurgling sound, like water flowing through a partially clogged
drain. In between came a prolonged, mournful whine, like a
spider spinning out a thread. It sounded like the person was
competing with the wailing of the wind.

A muffled announcement over the intercom.

"This is the Fulfilled Vow Parking Lot. In compliance with the divine revelation from the Venerable Bodhisattva Hanakumba, the gates shall now be closed."

"What on earth does that mean—'Fulfilled Vow Parking Lot'?"

"That's unusual—is that how it sounded to you?"

"I wonder if I heard wrong."

"It sounds to me like 'Chiang Mai Parking Lot.' "

"Why? Isn't Chiang Mai in Thailand or somewhere?"

"Evidently it sounds different to different people. It doesn't matter, does it? Neither the doctors nor the nurses seem to agree on a single theory."

"It's a strange broadcast."

"Because this is a hospital."

"Shouldn't we contact the nurse about that man who's in agony?"

"No, it's all right. Twenty minutes after the parking lot announcement is lights-out. The nurses do their last rounds just before that. . . ."

"It's impossible to sleep."

"During the day he does nothing but sleep, but when night comes, he starts making this racket."

"How aggravating."

As he predicted, two nurses came trotting noiselessly along and drew open the curtain around the bed by the door, on the other side of the room. A prune-faced old man gripped his IV pole with his nearly mummified fingers and shrieked like a cat at the moment of orgasm. He was reveling in Death's embrace. The nurses each took a side of the bed and pushed it out into the hall.

"After the lights are off they make him sleep in the hall."

"What's wrong with him?"

"Probably everything. His head, his heart . . ."

"Does he stand a chance?"

"Let's go out to the smoking lounge."

"I don't smoke."

"I want to smoke. Besides, I want to pay the escape artist and place our order. You must be starving."

"Can we meet him there?"

"It's the social center. For the patients. Even after curfew there's a light on there, and there's a TV—granted, the reception is poor—and a public phone and a bunch of weekly magazines and things. . . ."

"Who decides the channel?"

"You're a weirdo. You think of strange things. There's a system for channel selection in places like this. You bet money, and the winner takes his choice."

The smoking lounge was nearly directly across from the door. It was a small room, about twelve feet by fifteen feet. There were two tables covered with cigarette burns and two benches with thin sponge cushions, five metal folding chairs, a magazine rack overflowing with various weekly magazines, and in each corner, a brass ashtray on legs.

There were already six visitors puffing intently on cigarettes. Neolithic Man lit an imitation-gold-plated lighter with trembling fingers and introduced me. He described me simply as the new patient in the bed next to him, a poor guy who had been hospitalized for a concussion and had missed dinner. He didn't mention my name or occupation. That was understandable, since he didn't know them. But Neolithic Man's speech was effective. Everyone immediately became friendly toward me. They made room for me on the corner of a bench. They offered me cigarettes, which Neolithic Man promptly snatched before I could refuse them. Apparently the TV had already been claimed by someone. An extremely boisterous animation program was on. Everyone was in stitches. What a cheerful bunch of patients! Or are they cheerful because they're patients?

"Thanks for your help." Neolithic Man pressed the folded bills into the palm of a large man in a neck brace who had placed his metal chair squarely in front of the TV set. The man looked as though he suffered from gigantism. "A box of twelve. After this program is over will be fine."

Neck Brace chuckled, then turned around and flashed me a smile. He pointed to the TV and asked, "Do you like it?"

"I haven't seen this show before."

The patients around us exploded in laughter. Neck Brace laughed as uproariously as the rest. I couldn't tell whether they were clowning around or making fun of me. I sensed danger in the air.

"You said you want twelve. That means carp cakes, doesn't it?" The one who chimed in was a middle-aged man in a wheel-chair, wearing a bright-red gown and a red beret. He had been absorbed in a comic book depicting historical events, but he slapped the magazine shut. "You're the only one here who supports the carp cake shop. In this neighborhood the moon bun shop on the corner is the place to go. That's what everyone else thinks, right?"

"But they only give you ten."

"Their buns are heavier. Because they're bursting with bean jam."

"How often do you get a carp cake that's stuffed from head to tail with bean jam?"

"The moon bun has a long history. The secret is in the jam, not the crust."

"Idiots!" bellowed Neolithic Man. "Well, maybe you ought to try sword bars. Now, there's an elegant sweet. But you can make a whole meal out of carp cakes or moon buns. . . ."

"So what's it to you? The guy who's gonna eat it is the one who should choose." Wheelchair glared at me. "Why don't you assert yourself?"

Neolithic Man: "How can someone who's never eaten either of them make the decision? Moron! If you weren't confined to a wheelchair I'd knock your block off."

"I'd like to see you try. Go right ahead."

No sooner had he said this than he thrust out the stick that had been hanging on the side of his wheelchair. Neolithic Man just managed to dodge the attack.

"Such a violent criminal! Far worse than I expected. No wonder you're in here with broken bones."

Wheelchair brandished his stick and didn't flinch.

"And you talk like an ignoramus. You're downright uncouth."

Wheelchair spun around one hundred eighty degrees and deftly caught Neolithic Man's arm with the tip of his stick. It was obviously not a mere emotional outburst but a calculated performance. Even Neolithic Man backed off. Keeping a distance between himself and Wheelchair, he circled the table.

The animation ended and a commercial featuring an orangutan came on the TV. At the same time, an announcement came over the intercom at very low volume.

"It is now time to turn off the lights. Your cooperation is appreciated. Please turn off all lights. . . ."

Someone's excited voice: "God, I love this monkey!"

Someone's objection: "An orangutan isn't a monkey. It's an anthropoid."

"I love it! Look at those eyes—like he's been sobbing his heart out. . . ."

"He looks just like you."

"What a great face!"

That moaning grew louder. On the same side as the smoking lounge was a toilet, and next to that a shower stall, and between that and the emergency exit behind it was the old man's bed, pushed against the wall. At the end of the hallway was the nurses' station, so it didn't seem as though the man was being mistreated. He began making a whistling sound in his throat, and the note of entreaty in his moan gradually became more insistent. He sat up, drew up one knee, and suddenly spread his legs apart. His purplish penis, like a wizened eggplant, plopped down on the bed.

"I wish they'd do something for that guy." My tone of voice was inadvertently reproachful.

"They're doing all they can do," someone muttered.

One of the nurses who had been around a short while before returned from a treatment room in the back. A woman with pretty legs, she resembled a certain TV newscaster who spoke excellent English. She closed the old man's legs, tucked a blanket around them, and gently massaged his chest, where his respiratory muscles were heaving laboriously.

"Try to put up with it. This is why we tell you not to sleep during the day. Everyone wants to sleep now, so you mustn't bother them. There, you feel better now, don't you? The staff room is right over there, so there's no need to worry. Someone will come to you right away, anytime you call, so . . ."

Within moments his breathing became calm. I had never yielded so helplessly to anyone, so the nurse's tenderness had an intoxicating effect on me.

"I wonder if it's partly psychological; he seems to have become comfortable."

No one voiced agreement with me. The giant in the neck brace slowly lifted himself up.

"So carp cakes it is, eh?"

"That's already been decided, hasn't it?" blustered Neolithic Man.

"Do whatever the hell you please." Red Beret sank down into his canvas-seated wheelchair.

The escape artist got up. His height alone made his presence intimidating. Can such a conspicuous figure possibly succeed at escape work? He tossed the remote control onto the table, cracked his knuckles, and did some bending and stretching and a few toe stands.

When Neck Brace began leaving the smoking lounge, moving like a sleepwalker, the old man's fits recommenced, as if to foil his escape. The repeated convulsions and spasms of someone on the verge of asphyxia.

"Maybe these are his final moments."

"Don't count on it."

Wheelchair began rhythmically tapping his stick, as if he were beating on a little drum.

"Ratatat ratatat tat-tat ratatat . . ."

Another nurse, also wearing rubber-soled shoes, came running from a treatment room. She looks like someone else too. . . . The mole beneath her right eye, the mouth puckered as if she were sucking on a pickled plum . . . Who is it? Probably that popular Japanese folk singer.

A huge human shadow glided past me. Head bowed, the figure followed right behind the nurse and disappeared into the shower room. He was indeed an expert. He moved naturally, attracting no attention. His sly strategy was to use his conspicuous frame to his advantage. In another twenty to thirty minutes, will I be feasting on carp cakes? My mouth began watering so much that the base of my tongue burned.

T h e   b e h a v i o r of the nurse with the mole beneath her eye provided me with a splendid sense of continuity. As if she were following a written schedule, she efficiently took the old man's pulse, peered into the pupils of his eyes with a flashlight, pulled a motor out from beneath the bed, and connected it to an aspirator. She inserted a tube through his mouth and suctioned mucus from his windpipe. The sound was just like the one made by a siphon-style coffeemaker. Immediately his breathing became peaceful.

"Do you feel better? While I'm here, shall I wipe your back?"

The old man began wheezily making some appeal in the nurse's ear. I couldn't make out what he was saying, but the nurse evidently understood.

"It's all right. No one is angry. Look, they're all smiling." She ran her own comb through the old man's wispy hair and said, "Just a minute, okay?"

She took the washcloth by his pillow and ran to the shower room. No more than a few minutes could have passed since Neck Brace sneaked in there. He may be a pro, but he's botched things this time. I looked around and saw confusion or tension on every face.

No ruckus ensued. The nurse came out of the shower holding the hot, wet washcloth by its edges and shaking it to adjust the temperature. She gently raised the old man up, warmed his chest, then wiped his back from shoulders to waist. She worked lightly, diligently, varying her movements according to the old man's responses.

Suddenly tears welled up in me. It's hard to explain why. Astonishment that such incredible compassion should actually exist. I couldn't believe my eyes. Shame at my own coarseness. Maybe witnessing such selflessness wrings people's hearts until tears flow from their eyes.

The old man drifted off to sleep.

"Say, don't tear those leaves." A sturdy-looking doctor, like a wooden doll, stood there with feet planted apart. A placid but dry person, who seemed to have deposited his emotions elsewhere. "It's been put there by the hospital to have a soothing effect on everyone."

Apparently I was the one who was being reprimanded. I had been unconsciously digging my fingernails into the leaves of the rubber tree that stood in the corner of the smoking lounge.

"I'm sorry. I was just trying to see if it was real or plastic."

"That's no excuse."

"I quite agree."

Thunder rumbled a second time. It seemed very close by. The TV picture wavered and the lights flickered, but there wasn't a power failure. A sudden gust of wind, then on the roof a droning like a huge spinning top.

Again the old man began to groan. Without seeming a bit annoyed, the nurse with the mole began preparing the aspirator again.

"Doctor, you know . . .," Red Beret began mumbling, "thunder smells, doesn't it . . . a bit fishy, like semen . . ."

"The air is charged with negative ions."

"Do negative ions have an invigorating effect?"

"I've never heard such a thing."

The aspirator's motor whirred; the sound of a clogged water pipe clearing.

I impulsively called out to the doctor, who was leaving.

"What's wrong with that man?"

"Why?"

"Does he stand a chance of recovery?"

"That's no concern of a patient like yourself."

But he didn't seem particularly irritated. I realized that my behavior was inappropriate for a patient, but I persisted.

"Does he stand a chance of not dying?"

"Cut it out!" Neolithic Man grabbed my elbow and shook it.

"If you're referring to that moaning . . ." The doctor nodded and spoke calmly. "I know that it's disturbing to all of you, but it's not indicative of the gravity of his illness. Probably from childhood he was very timid and had somewhat of a persecution complex. So he keeps howling like that from a constant anxiety about being attacked."

"He'd make a good watchdog," said Neolithic Man, but no one laughed.

"Isn't 'death with dignity' appropriate for that sort of patient?"

"Don't you mean 'euthanasia'?"

"How are they different?"

"Doesn't that old fellow look human to you?"

"He does."

"Can you confidently claim that you have preserved more dignity than he?"

"But he really seems to be suffering. . . ."

Actually, the old man was already asleep. The nurse was massaging his toes one by one. His toothless mouth was open slightly; grotesque, yet smiling, he was gliding through a dream.

"Please don't damage the potted plant," said the doctor amiably, then he left. "Keep up the good work," he said to the nurse, then he looked back at me and spoke quickly. "What I was talking about was strictly 'death with dignity.' Euthanasia is not a medical issue; in my opinion, it's a form of murder."

The nurse followed the doctor and disappeared. For a while there was dead silence. No matter how violent the gale, it's mild compared to human moaning. The television was still on, but no one was in charge of it. The weather forecast finished and a commercial for a health drink came on. Neolithic Man lit his third cigarette. A young man who hadn't opened his mouth until then began speaking in a hoarse voice. Except for a growth on his chin, he looked healthier than anyone else.

"What the doctor just said can be interpreted in various

ways. . . . But frankly speaking, I can't stand this any longer. I've been on a rugby team for a long time, but I have no desire to die. Since coming here, my condition seems to have gotten worse, if anything. At night we don't sleep a wink, right? If death with dignity is out of the question, then there's no other choice but euthanasia, is there? The old fellow has absolutely no chance of recovery. They're only prolonging his agony."

"The doctor didn't say that. He said that it's the police who handle euthanasia." Red Beret rapped the tip of his stick on the floor. "Assisting a suicide, forced double suicide, murder by contract—they're all clear-cut criminal offenses. Am I right?"

My throat was dry. I removed an ice chip from the ice pack around my jaw and popped it into my mouth. A cool current of resolve rippled from my jaw to the area between my eyebrows.

"Do you know about the 'Japanese Euthanasia Club's Organizational Meeting'? As a matter of fact, an acquaintance of mine is running it."

"I said cut that out!" Neolithic Man rebuked me sharply. No one said a word.

The door to the shower room opened and the giant in the neck brace appeared, grinning impishly. His body seems buoyant, like smoke or balloons, as if it's all volume and no mass. He held the thin wooden box up to show us. Before I had a chance to thank him, he thanked me very politely. As well he might. A delivery service with a thousand-yen fee isn't a bad sideline.

I bought some canned coffee and carried the box of carp

cakes back to my bed. I removed two cakes from among the closely packed dozen, set them on the box lid, and passed them over to Neolithic Man, as promised.

"You eat it starting from the tip of the tail. The tail is the vital part."

Not bad at all. I've always loved bean jam. But given a choice, I prefer chunky jam to the smooth kind. Maybe I should have asked for the moon buns. . . .

I had just polished off the second carp, tail first. Again the anguished moaning, like a dog's distant howling, came from the old man in the corridor. Is it really just a persecution complex? Isn't it physical torment manifesting itself on the psychological level?

The student with the tumor on his chin peeked in nervously.

"I'm sorry to bother you while you're eating. I can't take it any longer. Please contact the Euthanasia Club. I beg you. It's not just a nuisance. I can't bear to watch. It wouldn't be murder, just a matter of killing someone who's already dead. Don't you agree?"

"It's risky; it's definitely risky."

Neolithic Man bit into the tail of a carp cake, and as he squeeezed the jam out of the hole and slurped it up, he started wiggling his lower body like a seal. Student began defending his position.

"Idealism aside, when we consider this as a practical problem, isn't euthanasia actually a humane solution? In America the Supreme Court has recently approved mercy killing for monkeys used in scientific experiments."

"Human beings aren't monkeys."

"If I find out that this tumor on my chin is malignant, I'll choose euthanasia without a moment's hesitation. As far as I'm concerned, being in such a wretched condition doesn't qualify as living."

Well now, which of them do I agree with? If the "radish sprouts" on my legs are diagnosed as an incurable disease, will I choose euthanasia? If it simply means that the "radish sprouts" can't be exterminated, I can always conceal them with socks or something. But what if my skin continues its metamorphosis into a vegetable patch? What if the sprouts spread to my eyes, nose, ears, and mouth, then infiltrate my urethra and anus, begin thriving inside my body, and I finally turn into a giant plant, like an algae ball. . . . Obviously, euthanasia would be the only choice. Suicide probably ought to be recognized as a human right.

The intermittent shrieking in the corridor intensified. Then it trembled, paused, and subsided, like a siren receding into the distance. Finally, the aspirator motor began to whir.

"I've had it. It must be torture for the patient, and the nurses are pathetic. The purpose of medical treatment is to restore a person's humanity, isn't it?"

"Even so . . ." Neolithic Man crammed the entire shell of carp cake, from which he had sucked all the jam, into his mouth.

"All right. I'll phone and ask about it for you." I was picturing myself metamorphosed into an algae ball. "But I can take no responsibility for the outcome."

I have a knack for never forgetting a name or a phone number that I've heard. In cases like this, my memory is a liability. I took the remaining five carp cakes and returned to

I felt him hesitate slightly before replying. I rushed to elaborate, but he silenced me firmly. No, spare me the details. I don't want to be an accomplice, you know. I'll just teach you some techniques for devising the perfect crime for your particular situation. There's only one condition: that the victim isn't too attached to his life. . . .

"That I can guarantee one hundred percent. His breathing is feeble. He's moaning constantly."

The men straining their ears to hear seemed to sense that the deal was progressing smoothly, and among the tense faces subtle differences began to appear. Expectation . . . fear . . . confusion . . . curiosity . . .

"Of course, I'm not asking you to take responsibility for the ethical issues. I understand. No one in the world could possibly regret the guy's death. Right now about ten people are crowded around this phone, but if there were even one objection I couldn't make this phone call. I myself don't want to risk anything so dangerous. It's all right. I don't know how old he is but probably around eighty. It's not that he's all wrinkled but he's brittle; his skin is like persimmon paper. You don't know what persimmon paper is? That's right, he's like a well-preserved mummy. . . . I don't know whether he has heart trouble, or liver trouble, or maybe cancer. . . ."

His reply was brief. This type of victim was the easiest to away with. But he definitely wanted us to provide something so he could develop a formal association out of the sale at the organizational meeting. In addition, he would need money for the drugs and the executioner's signature and official stamp, or else his thumbprint. . . .

"So to get right down to it, how much do you want?"

the smoking lounge; a bluish haze of cigarette smoke
tled over the ceiling.

"I have twenty-two calls left on my telephone
dent took the card from his shirt pocket.

The old man drifted into sleep. After makin
the nurse was back in the staff room, I decisively
buttons on the phone. It began ringing. On the thir
one answered. A man's voice. I felt relieved. Evid
nothing going on to prevent him from answering

"Mr. Killer? Do you know who this is? T
everything. You even took care of my hospital
If only the clinic I first went to would send
cards . . ."

Master Killer launched into a long-winded s
Understandably so. If it weren't for his bungled
my dislocated jaw, I wouldn't have landed in t
patients in the smoking lounge were staring e
phone receiver, looking as though they were ab
screams of excitement. How can I broach th
thanasia? Doesn't merely discussing such a
plotting a crime?

"How is she?"

Tonight she's out drawing blood again
tenacious. But I guess tonight her turf is re
in such high spirits; she even put on eye sh
out. Doesn't it bother you, Killer? I would

"By the way, can I ask you somethin
hanging on that glass door, you know the
euthanasia—the 'Euthanasia Club's Org
. . . I have a question about that."

Ten thousand yen in financial assistance and ten thousand yen for drugs, a total of twenty thousand yen. It seemed expensive, and at the same time it seemed cheap. Probably it wasn't expensive. I didn't need to do any coaxing; in no time there was a stack of thousand-yen bills on the table.

"He said that within the next five minutes he'd deliver the drug to the back entrance in a red mini-van."

Wheelchair counted the bills on the table, gave them a satisfied snap with his finger, and said, "Twenty-three thousand yen. . . . If we're going to hire our regular expert to pick up the drug . . ." He removed one bill and held it out to Neck Brace. "What should we do with the other two thousand yen?"

"That'll be the payment for the one who executes the crime. I don't know what sort of drug it is, but in any case, someone will have to administer it to the old man."

"He said the drug goes down easily. It's like malt syrup. It's made from the root of wolfsbane. . . ."

From the corner came a voice.

"Isn't that all the rage these days? Something like that will be discovered right away, won't it?"

"As long as we don't arouse any suspicion, there won't be a forensic autopsy." I wanted to stay out of it if possible, but I couldn't very well keep silent. "Because the immediate cause of death isn't poisoning but asphyxiation. First we use the wolfsbane to cause muscle paralysis. Then we casually cover his nose and mouth with a wet cloth. His last moments will be peaceful."

"Who's going to do it?" Neolithic Man glared belligerently into one pair of eyes after another.

"Obviously we'll have to draw lots. Everyone made a donation, so . . ." Student's voice had grown steadily hoarser.

A man with a short crew cut who was wearing a Japanese kimono and a pair of sunglasses sprayed out some saliva. "Someone's honking a horn."

"I'll go see." Neck Brace rose lightly, like a wisp of smoke.

"I don't want to die . . . ," sighed someone, somewhere.

Student tore a sheet off the calendar on the wall (three more days to the end of the month), spread it out on the table, and began preparing the lottery. As he cut each fateful strip of paper, he blew on it and muttered some invocation.

I slowly bit into my sixth carp cake. I craved a ripe tomato.

There was a tense interval, then finally the door to the shower room opened and Neck Brace came tiptoeing back. He held out a container wrapped in vinyl that was about the size of a thirty-five-millimeter film cartridge.

"He looked like a foreigner. But his Japanese was too good. Is he half and half?"

"He's American."

"Amazing. He says he'll pay you a visit tomorrow."

"Well then, it's time to draw." Student thrust out his chest and glanced around the group.

"I'll pass," said Neck Brace matter-of-factly, and headed for his room.

"But it's the drawing to decide the executioner."

"Count me out." The words no one else dared to utter. Was it courage or insensitivity . . . ?

Suddenly they all got up as if it had nothing to do with them and nonchalantly returned to their beds.

"Don't take it hard." Neolithic Man placed his hand on

the shoulder of the crestfallen student, picked up the little bot-
tle from the table, and pressed it into his hand. "Come on,
don't dilly-dally. Now is the time, while no one's watching. The
washcloth is hanging right over the old man's bed rail. . . ."

"You're a sneaky bunch."

"The drug takes effect immediately, so as soon as you give
it to him you can put the cloth over his face."

"You're cruel, the two of you!"

Neolithic Man and I left the sobbing youth by himself
and returned to our beds. Fifteen minutes later, Student appeared at the foot of my bed.

"Is it over?"

He just kept blubbering. I held the box out to him. He
finally quieted down and gently sank his teeth into the tail of
the carp cake he'd taken.

"So sweet . . ."

A blustering gale. Inside that wind, the sound of another
wind. Surely it's a festival throng.

CHAPTER SEVEN
the kidnapper

In the past kidnappers hunted for children
But these days children hunt for kidnappers

A violent gale. A northeasterly wind driving against the ward at nearly a right angle. The frictional sound of atmospheric streams of different velocities chafing high in the sky. An analog phonograph playing music created by the striated ground. A rich stew of information. Using my auditory nerve system as a high-precision analyzer, I tried to separate the sounds.

Sounds beckoning me, voices calling me . . .

Is that a train station announcement? The vibration of a

cheap loudspeaker announcing a train's arrival or departure. But didn't someone say that? It must have been Neolithic Man. That there's no train station windward of here. There are neither farms nor villages. Just a sandstone hill that barely manages to survive, thanks to a grove of misshapen pine trees. The northeast wind rises from the ocean and comes over the hill blowing on conch shells.

I couldn't give up. I climbed off the bed and walked down the aisle. I poked a finger through the window blinds and peered out. Dreadful pitch-blackness. Not a single city light was visible in the total darkness, let alone a train station.

Yet I kept staring out longingly. Particles of light began floating in the air. It must be an illusion. Don't they say that ninety percent of apparitions are just cedar trees in the darkness?

An even stranger sound rushed by beneath the eaves of the ward.

"A message from the Fulfilled Vow Parking Lot. The parking lot is now closed. The reception desk for donations to the Venerable Bodhisattva Hanakumba will be closing shortly. Please bring your donations at once."

A chorus of howling monkeys with colds provide accompaniment: *"Help me, help me, help me, please. Please, please, won't you help me, please. . . ."*

It's a small clue. Evidently the Riverbank of Sai and this hospital aren't totally unrelated. Virtually everything seems to be interconnected and entangled. I have a hunch that if I went somewhere I could even meet the child-demons of the Riverbank again. What haunts me more than anything is that young girl in the dirty size-L undershirt. I have absolutely no tactile memory of her. I want to touch her. I want to confirm the resilience of her skin with my fingers.

"What's wrong? Can't you sleep?" One of Neolithic Man's eyes was peering through an opening in his bed curtain.

"It bothers me."

"The old guy who took the wolfsbane? You can relax. He died in peace, without a peep, while you were asleep. It was an enviably peaceful death."

"I was sleeping?"

"You were singing."

"What sort of song?"

"Like something a ghost would mumble in its sleep."

I grabbed the curtain around Neolithic Man's bed and flung it open. I had no ulterior motive. I just felt rather lonely, and I wanted to sit on the corner of his bed or something. His reaction was unexpectedly violent. He snarled and shoved me away.

"Idiot! Say something before you open it."

He was sitting cross-legged, with the bottom of his gown hiked up and his lower body exposed. Swirls of stiff hair crawled up from his shins to his inner thighs, encircled his genitals, ran up to his navel, and sprouted into chest hair. What intrigued me even more were those pornographic photos, strewn around his knees, that I had seen once before. In spite of them, Neolithic Man's penis was buried in pubic hair as glossy as iron and showed no sign of an erection. Maybe he's already done the deed, with the help of the photos.

"I'm sorry."

"Son of a bitch. You've humiliated me." Suddenly he lowered his voice. "I can't get it up."

Caught off guard by this entirely unexpected confession, I barely managed a lame response.

"Maybe it's because you used your daughter as a model. They say human beings have an instinctive aversion to incest. . . ."

"I said I'm impotent! Son of a bitch . . ." Neolithic Man groaned through clenched teeth. He stuffed the skirt of his gown between his thighs, gathered up the pornographic photos, and said, "You're sneering at me, aren't you?"

"Sneering? Of course not. From the outside, you seem perfectly normal."

"Give me a break. Put yourself in my position. It's awful—looking at naked women and not feeling anything. I don't feel anything, so I don't want to look. But even the covers of weekly magazines are full of nudes. It's like my nose is plugged up."

"Doesn't it simplify things? I practically envy you. Take me—I'm always worried that I might be a sex maniac. . . . Nylon stockings, a slightly crushed jam bun wrapped in a cherry leaf—one glimpse and I react. . . ."

"And you're griping! I'm seriously thinking of having an operation."

"I wonder if it's so crucial . . ."

"I'm missing out."

Neolithic Man picked up the stack of Polaroid photos as if they were a deck of cards and placed them in front of me. Right on top was an incredibly obscene one. Of course, maybe it only looked obscene to me. Actually, it had attracted me the first time I saw it, but I had restrained myself from picking it up for fear that he'd read my mind. The male partner was not in the photograph. It was a picture of a headless girl. One of her knees was slightly raised. Ribs visible between her breasts. Only her thighs were voluptuous; the richness of their inner flesh was nearly palpable. Near the left thigh joint was a small pinkish birthmark. Shaped like Sado Island. Two fingers touching the wispy pubic hair. The edges of her inner labia were visible; they looked just like thin slices of mushroom. My heart skipped a beat, then trembled like jelly.

"Take them."

All I had left in my pocket was a thousand-yen bill and some small change. I can't very well spend this thousand yen. But I want what I want. The photo has an allure for me that surpasses mere lust.

"Will you accept a trade?"

"A trade?"

"I'll give you back the other ones."

I took a deep breath and studied his face. I have to have it, no matter what.

"Never mind. I'll give it to you as a bonus."

I immediately pulled a photo out of my pocket and switched it with the one on the top of the stack.

"Sleight of hand, huh?"

"It's a shocking photo. . . . Is it really your own daughter?"

"It's a way to make pocket money. A quick thousand yen for one photo."

"It's doing that sort of thing that makes you impotent."

"If you want them, take them all. I didn't like doing it myself. I said go ahead and take them all."

I was skeptical, but I thought I'd better take them before he changed his mind. I divided the stack in two and stuck half in my shirt pocket and half in my pants pocket. I took out the thousand-yen note and spread it out on the spot where the photos had been.

"I thought you were broke."

"No, but I can't spend this thousand yen on those. There's something I want more than anything else."

"What?"

"Information."

"I'd rather not milk you any more than I have."

"Introduce me. To the big guy in the neck brace. The one who went to buy the carp cakes for us a while ago. . . ."

"What do you want to know?"

"The after-hours exit."

"If it's tissues or a ballpoint pen that you need . . ."

"I just want to get out for a bit."

"Planning a getaway?"

"I'll be back. I promise."

" 'Promise'? You don't owe me anything. He's next door in Bed Number Four."

I scooped up the thousand-yen note and pocketed it; I was amazed at my own agility. Neolithic Man raised his outspread hand beside his ear and waved bye-bye to me like a baby. Then he extended the back scratcher and pulled the curtain shut.

I went back to my bed and looked for my shoes. They had been on the spot on the floor that was perpendicular to my left elbow. Where did they go? I got down on all fours and peeked under the bed. My shoes came crawling out. Along with them came Student, fingers pressed to his lips. He grabbed my pants cuffs and put my shoes on for me. He was a peculiar guy. His smile twisted into a kind of plea, and again he pressed his fingers firmly to his lips. When I began to leave, he slouched down and followed me.

We went out to the corridor. Except for the smoking lounge, everything was shrouded in an amber-tinted darkness. The slanting beam of light ahead of us came from the lamp in the nurses' station.

Suddenly I turned around and confronted him before he had a chance to say anything.

"What do you want?"

"Take me with you. Please."

"Where?"

"You're escaping, aren't you?"

"I'm just going out for some fresh air."

"I'll do it for free."

"Do what?"

"Show you the secret passage."

"Then you don't need me. You can make your own getaway."

"I'm scared."

"Of what?"

"There's a nest of huge rats. And spiders . . ."

"Big deal."

"I have a heart condition. I can't tolerate shock."

"Where are you headed?"

"Nowhere in particular. I just can't stand being here. After all, I'm a murderer, aren't I?"

I didn't want to talk about murder. I was in a sadistic

mood, so I decided to give him a hard time. I pulled the stack of pornographic photos out of my pants pocket and turned them over, one by one.

"This is what you're really after, isn't it? One of them? Two? Or don't you want this sort of thing?"

"I want it."

Student's voice quavered. His candor made me relent.

"Here you go. I'll give you three. What a deal."

Naturally I kept my favorite, the girl with the birthmark on her inner thigh.

"It's good of you. These are worth fifteen hundred yen even before markup. That's quite a sum. Afterwards I'll admire them at leisure."

A blue lamp that said "Emergency Exit."

We tiptoed down the stairs, Student leading the way. We made it to the lower basement without running into anyone. At the bottom of the last staircase was an emergency flashlight that I pulled out of its socket.

"The ventilator behind that oil burner. It's safe because the burner isn't used during the summer, but because of that, there are big rats living there. Those red tails terrify me. . . ."

The vent was a tunnel about the length of four oil drums joined together. Actually, I'm not fond of rats myself. But I didn't want to show any weakness. I switched on the flashlight and illuminated the inside of the passage. Shovel marks on the hard tunnel walls. The black sheen of mineral oil. I can't imagine such delicate creatures as rats building their nests here.

"Here I go."

Student grabbed on to my belt. I leaned forward and scurried through without stopping, at times dropping to my knees.

I thought I was doing well, but Student sounded like a construction worker because of the hobnails on his heels. I hate this clumsy type.

Suddenly a gale so violent that my upper body shook. As soon as we emerged, we were on the ground.

We were greeted by an announcement, as if someone had been expecting us.

"This is a message from the Fullfilled Vow Parking Lot. The reception desk for donations to the Venerable Bodhisattva Hanakumba will be closing shortly. Please bring your donations at once."

"You heard 'Bodhisattva Hanakumba,' didn't you?"

"Hanakumba? He said 'Bodhisattva Hanako,' didn't he?"

"That's absurd. . . ."

Contrary to how it sounded from the hospital room window, the announcement did not seem to be coming from the windward direction.

"But these days Hanako's ghost is making regular appearances."

"Where's the sound coming from?"

"From the west; across the river, parallel to the ward . . ."

I pressed him, just to make sure. "Not from the windward direction, right?"

"That's right."

Reassured by his assertion, I began walking west, parallel to the ward.

"There's a hint of sulfur in this wind, isn't there?"

"Do you think so?"

"I'm certain it's sulfur."

"The parking lot is closed."

"You can go where you please. I'm not asking you to keep me company."

"Anyway, I'll cross the bridge."

For a while we walked along the ward in silence.

"I'm sure it's 'Hanakumba.' "

"Were you working for some company?"

"I still am, unless I've been fired."

"What sort of work were you doing?"

"I was supposed to be developing new products for an office supply company."

"Like what?"

"A kangaroo notebook."

"That sounds interesting."

"Why? I hate it when people go along with things for no reason."

"Don't you like kangaroos?"

"No one has managed to devise a method of distinguishing one from another. They say they lack individuality. Kind of like you, don't you think?"

"I ate kangaroo once. It's called 'jump steak.' Come to think of it, it *was* bland, like chicken thigh meat. So you think I lack individuality, like a kangaroo?"

"How would I know?"

Suddenly his voice rose to a shrill pitch. "But I'm not ordinary anymore. Because I'm a murderer."

"I told you to forget it. That was a group decision; you weren't the only one who wanted to kill him."

"What's the point of human life?"

"We're alive because we're alive. There's no particular purpose."

"That can't be. There has to be some meaning."

"Even if there's no meaning, people eagerly pile up life insurance. We're alive just because we don't want to die."

"That's awful, that way of thinking. . . ." His voice caught, and he sniffled noisily. "Once a person dies, he can't die again."

"Obviously. If you could commit suicide in hell, it wouldn't be hell."

"How can you come out with such unpleasant jokes?"

"Quit whining."

"I'm a murderer."

"That old man didn't die for the first time. Before you put the wet cloth over his face he was already in hell."

"Cruel, you're too cruel."

"I feel like I've been in hell for a long time, and I haven't even died yet. Just the other day, my dead mother and I nearly came to blows. . . ."

We arrived at the end of the ward. Student collapsed limply against the wall, then sank to his knees. He buried his face in his hands and began to sob. It was less restrained than sobbing; he seemed barely able to keep from wailing. Close by, a door hinge creaking in the wind. We were lucky to have the emergency lamp. In the darkness we might not have been able to make out the exit in the iron-framed wire-mesh fence.

"Don't leave me!" Student sprang to his feet.

"You can cry to your heart's content. Our destinations are different."

"Well, at least we can go together as far as the parking lot. . . ."

We crossed a bridge over a narrow irrigation ditch and

came to a two-lane paved road. The only lights visible were from the windows of the ward behind us and from a cluster of low buildings, far to our left. Directly across the road, two iron posts. A chain stretched between them. To their right, a shed trimmed in garish blue paint; it looked like the oversized telephone booths you see at amusement parks. Have we finally arrived at the Fulfilled Vow Parking Lot?

But there was no light on in the shed and, naturally, no sign of any attendant.

"I wonder if the desk taking donations to the Bodhisattva Hanakumba has closed too."

I glanced back at Student, not really expecting a reply.

"That's just a recording. It comes on automatically every hour, they say."

"Then what about the 'Help Me! Chorus'?"

"I have no idea about that. . . . Shall we go in and have a look? Most of the parked cars have been abandoned and their registrations have expired. They're cars that patients came to the hospital in. Visitors hardly ever come, and if a patient dies, his car probably just stays here. But I've heard that on this side close to the entrance there are quite a few that are still running. . . . Shall we look for one?"

"Wouldn't that be theft?"

"Apparently even the junkyard won't come to haul them away; you're doing them a favor by stealing one."

Suddenly, among the abandoned cars, an incongruous iron structure came crawling clumsily toward us. No doubt about it; it's my bed. Student doesn't seem to notice it yet. In this gale, the squeaking of the wheels probably isn't audible unless you strain to hear it.

Careful to avoid shining the flashlight on it, I egged Student on.

"When you're feeling anxious about something, there's nothing better than a late-night drive. Besides, compared to murder, stealing an abandoned car is the most minor of misdemeanors. How about that Toyota over there? Even the tire treads are in good condition."

"I don't like blue cars. But if the key is in the ignition, I guess we can't be choosy. . . ."

I handed him the emergency lamp and helped him release the chain at the exit. I was trying to distract him.

"I hear that if you go north on this road there's a pine grove on a hill and beyond that is the ocean."

"They say in the past there was a bathing beach there, and a train made a round trip there three times a day on a single-track line."

"Isn't that a sound from the past drifting here on the wind . . .?"

"If we're going to take a midnight jaunt, I'd like to go to the city."

Just as Student got into the blue station wagon, my bed came lumbering up to the roadside. I rolled onto it, belly down. As I brought my face to the pillow, I caught a whiff of my own odor. Instead of weeping, I sneezed.

Student apparently gave up on tagging along with me. That was the last I heard of him.

T h e b e d b e g a n running against the wind. It seemed to be trying to use the wind's lift to reduce its weight. Behind me I could hear the feeble, intermittent whirring of its starter.

Wind swelled, waves surged. I had to keep my face wrapped in the blanket in order to breathe. But I felt certain that I was approaching my destination.

I have no sensation of moving swiftly, but it seems like the bed is running on rails, swaying slightly from side to side. I had the same feeling when we were racing through the underground tunnel toward the canal. While I was waiting on a side track, a miniature amusement park train passed, going in the other direction; wasn't there a girl with sloping eyes riding on that? Maybe it's her voice that's wafting here on this wind, beckoning to me. It's confusing; I have to devise a code.

Sloping-eyes A . . . Sloping-eyes B . . . Sloping-eyes C . . .

Obviously, A is the nurse whom I first met at the urology clinic and later met again. B is the little girl on the miniature train whom I've just recalled. C of course is one of the child-demons who was chanting on the Riverbank of Sai. An inscrutable mystery. The nagging suspicion that A, B, and C are one and the same person. If she actually is the same person, and I met her at widely spaced intervals, then it's not strange that she should appear somewhat different each time. If I can meet B here, I definitely want to ask her about the reddish birthmark shaped like Sado Island on her inner thigh.

Close by, a bell sounded; that was clearly no illusion. Simultaneously, an announcement over a loudspeaker.

"The last outbound train is arriving. Please step back behind the white line and wait."

A shrill whistle. Then the wheels screeched and the bed came to a halt. I pulled the blanket off my head. Immediately, the howling of the wind stopped, as if I had put earplugs in my ears. My ears had sensed correctly; the bed had arrived at

a dark station platform. The place was dimly lit, probably because the station was no longer in use. It was teeming with
voices and footsteps, but there was not a person in sight. It's
more like a ghost station than a station no longer in service.

In the middle of the platform was a waiting room boarded
up with cedar planks, and through the dirty window glass I
could see a naked lightbulb, probably about forty watts, dangling from the ceiling. That seemed to be the only light around.

"You made it on time."

A diffident, sweet voice. It wasn't A and it wasn't C. The
waiting room window was unbolted and opened outward. A
female with sloping eyes leaned out and waved her hand. I've
seen that wave before. It is B, after all.

"On time for what?"

I scrambled off the bed and pushed down the pornographic photos that were sticking out of my shirt pocket.

"Don't you know? The circus is coming."

"The circus?"

"They say a kidnapper is coming with it too."

"A kidnapper?"

"You wouldn't happen to be the kidnapper, would you?"

"You must be joking."

"He's supposed to tell me who I am."

"I wish someone would tell me who *I* am."

"Won't you come in and have some tea?"

But the door of the waiting room was securely padlocked.
B stepped back from the window, crooked her finger, and made
a gesture as if she were fishing me up. Is she telling me to
enter through the window? In the middle of the waiting room

was a rusty firewood stove. Many winters must have passed since it had been used. Wooden benches along the walls, facing each other. On one bench a sleeping bag was spread out. Sloping-eyes B sat down on the edge of that bench, peered into a hand mirror, and reapplied her lipstick. It's definitely B. The gaudy lipstick color. I remember how the other time, too, it made a strangely vivid impression on me.

Beside the stove, a wooden shipping crate. Blue flames rose from a camping burner, where a small kettle began making noise. Two tin cups and bags of black tea.

B switched the mirror to her other hand. Printed in white letters on the back of the mirror was "JAL." She began combing her hair slowly. All of her actions belied her childish face. Maybe this girl is A's younger sister who disappeared. Come to think of it, the fact that she's so preoccupied with kidnappers might be significant. This girl isn't afraid of kidnappers; she's waiting for one. And this makeup of hers too—isn't it meant for seducing a kidnapper?

I started to ask about the birthmark on her inner thigh, but checked myself.

The water boiled. She placed a tea bag into one of the cups and poured the water in.

"Would you like cookies or pound cake?"

"Either is fine."

B reached under the bench and drew out a clothes basket woven in rattan.

"Change your clothes. Make yourself comfortable. . . . The bath is at the station."

"You seem to have been waiting here for a long time."

"Yes, it's been long, very long. . . ."

She stepped over my outstretched legs and went out the window. Her knee brushed against my lips. I caught a glimpse of her armpit. Its childishness made it all the more provocative.

"Actually, I'm kind of hungry. . . . Just a light snack would be fine."

"It looks like the circus is late again. Let's get something to eat while we're watching it. Would you like a beer?"

"Thanks."

As I watched B vanish into the darkness far down on the platform, I jiggled the tea bag in the cup and sipped the tea, heedless of burning my tongue. The sting of the hot liquid stunned me into a vivid realization of my situation.

From what age is consensual intercourse legal?

Anyway, I can't very well use the clothes basket. And if the clothes basket is off limits, I certainly can't use the bath. Neolithic Man's sadness must have been like this. I stuck my hand under one of my pants cuffs. I felt some minor changes, but the "radish sprouts" seemed as lush as ever. I went beneath the naked light-bulb and quickly rolled up a pants cuff. A handful of plants scattered over the floor—some that had withered and others that had just begun to wither. But new growth had replaced the old; it wasn't as if I'd been relieved of the "radish sprouts." The plants swayed gracefully in the breeze. They were whiter, finer, and longer than before; that was the only difference.

I yanked down my pants cuff in sheer frustration. Even the pornographic photos in my pocket now seemed revolting and futile.

The sound of a little drum, drifting on the wind. Faltering notes, played by a trumpet.

"Listen! You hear it, don't you? It sounds like the circus has arrived."

Sloping-eyes B was standing by the window. She was precariously holding out a can of beer, some pound cake, and a brown rice bun in a wrapper. The bun was scalding hot. She must have heated it in a microwave oven. You can't heat rice buns properly in a microwave. The temperature rises, but the middle of the bread stays undone. Is she slipshod? Or is she so fervently waiting for her kidnapper that she eats coarse fare without even noticing that it's coarse?

I sipped the beer, stuck my head out the window, and strained my ears.

"Listen! The rails are humming."

"You can't be serious." Naturally, I was alarmed. "My bed is standing at the platform. Is it going to be smashed?"

"I hear music too."

B kept staring at me intently. She narrowed her sloping eyes and peered steadily into my pupils. Is she trying to hypnotize me? Or has she been hypnotized by me? I peeled the wrapper off the bun, blew on it, and broke it in half. Inside was a bit of bean jam. The bun didn't have any hard part; the whole thing was light and puffy. Considerable skill is necessary to achieve this effect. First you have to sprinkle water lightly over the surface. Then there's the matter of timing. It's best to heat the bun twice, very briefly each time. Mastering a microwave oven takes intuition and plenty of experience. B seems to have settled into life here and grown pretty accustomed to it.

"What sort of music?"

"You ought to know."

Her eyes were full of yearning. What should I do? Go along with her misunderstanding and continue to play the role of kidnapper? If a misunderstanding makes the girl happy, I'm perfectly willing to comply. The only hitch is that I don't know enough about kidnappers to sustain the charade.

"Isn't it your imagination?"

"What's that song? It's by Pink Floyd . . . the one you used to hear at the circus. . . . 'Echoes,' isn't it?"

An uncanny coincidence. I know nothing about circuses, but Pink Floyd's "Echoes" is one of my favorite pieces. On nights when I was sleepy but couldn't fall asleep because my nerves were on edge, the song worked wonders. Music to tranquilize madness, if you will.

I nibbled on the bun and drank the beer. The only sound was the ardor in B's gaze.

Suddenly a warning whistle pealed and a two-car train glided up to the platform. It was garishly decorated, like that miniature amusement park train I'd seen. Around its windows were exotic geometric designs drawn in noctilucent or fluorescent paint.

"Can't you signal it? It's going to crash!"

The collision happened before I could finish speaking. The train was already moving slowly, and the weight difference between the two objects was so great that the impact was gentler than I'd expected. But the bed began writhing and shrieking pathetically, and it disintegrated before my eyes into a heap of metal scraps. Magic carpet ripped apart. The cyclical tale has finally come to a halt. Is this the end of the line for me? Until now, each time I was on the brink of disaster, the bed played a role in my rescue by whisking me from one dream to another. . . .

Unfortunately, B seemed oblivious to my fears. She pointed at my demolished bed and snickered. Her reaction seemed on the one hand purely innocent, and on the other, like a hunter's sign of victory over his quarry.

Six automatic doors opened at once. No one disembarked. But I thought I saw a herd of small gray animals rush out. Jumping at amazing speed, they crossed the platform and scattered into the darkness. They're too small for kangaroos; maybe they're wallabies. Again, perfect silence.

B was responding to something with her whole body. She was waving her arm vigorously in a gesture of welcome.

"Can you see it?"

"Do you think I can't?"

"Isn't it too dark?"

"I can see it."

So she claimed, but she seemed uncertain.

"You're right. If I strain my eyes, I feel as if I can see it."

"Really?"

B peered deeply into my eyes, over my can of beer. She seemed to be trying to further reduce the distance between us by pressing me to agree.

"Why would I lie?"

"Then please clap for them."

I set my beer and bread down on the windowsill, and synchronizing my applause with hers, I clapped until my hands hurt.

"That's enough." Suddenly B's whole body went limp and

she stopped clapping. "No one is here. . . . Business is bad. They say circuses are a thing of the past."

"Are we the only spectators?"

"You can hear the music, can't you?"

"What kind of music?"

"Right now it's only drums. When 'Echoes' begins, it's my turn to perform. Wait here, won't you? Don't go away. I used to be an official member of the troupe. After that, there will be a show with mirrors. . . . Would you like to hear it?"

"What?"

"My song."

"The Riverbank of Sai song?"

"Hardly."

"Of course I want to hear it."

"Listen! It's beginning."

I couldn't hear anything, but her body transmitted the rhythm to me.

Puckering her mouth up into a little drum, she tapped her cheek with her finger and kept the beat. If it weren't for the "radish sprouts," I would have taken her in my arms then and there. Why must I endure such loneliness? Even though this radiant smile is brimming with delights . . .

A childish, sweet voice. A coquettish, sidelong glance. She knelt down and began softly singing.

> *Long ago kidnappers hunted for children,*
> *But every maze was marked with a number*
> *And there was nowhere left to hide them.*
> *So now all the kidnappers have retired*

and children roam in search of them.
Now children hunt for kidnappers.

No one can remember when life began.
No one can recognize when life ends.
But the festival begins
And the festival ends.
The festival is not human life
And human life is not a festival.
That's why kidnappers come along.
When the festival begins,
At dusk a kidnapper will arrive.

Several small human figures entered my peripheral vision. Skulking through the darkness, they skirted the waiting room, carrying a carton about the size of a large refrigerator. They seemed to be mumbling to themselves, but they were chanting softly, supplying the lower register of B's song. . . .

(Help me, help me, help me, please. Please, please, won't you help me, please)

The group in sleeveless undershirts placed the carton beneath the window and dragged me down from the window. They rolled me up like a wet rag and tried to stuff me into the box through its side opening. The reason I didn't particularly resist was that B herself seemed to be cooperating with the child-demons and lending them a hand. Besides, I ought to be able to rip open a cardboard box with my finger anytime, if I feel like it. . . .

B went on singing, her voice like a rusty flute.

> *Beneath the little window facing north,*
> *At the base of the bridge,*
> *At the foot of the mountain path,*
>
> *Afterwards,*
> *The kidnapper who arrived too late,*
> *The kidnapper I could not meet,*
> *The kidnapper I loved.*
>
> *The kidnapper who arrived too late,*
> *The kidnapper I could not meet,*
> *The kidnapper I loved.*

(Help me, help me, help me, please. Please, please, won't you help me, please)

The box was no ordinary carton. It was tough and resilient, like hard plastic.

On the front of it was a peephole. An opening the size of a mail slot.

I peeked out. I saw myself from behind. That self was peeking out of a peephole too.

He seemed terrified.

I was as terrified as he seemed.

It was dreadful.

Excerpt from a newspaper article:

A corpse was found on the premises of a train station no longer in service. On the man's shins were several slash marks that appeared to have been made by a razor. The wounds, evidently made with some hesitation, seemed to have been self-inflicted. It is unlikely that these were the cause of death. The incident is being investigated both as an accident and as a criminal case. Despite intensive efforts, the victim's identity has not yet been established.

a   n o t e   a b o u t   t h e   a u t h o r

Abe Kōbō was born in Tokyo in 1924, grew up in Manchuria, and returned to Japan in his early twenties. While studying medicine at Tokyo University, he began writing fiction. By 1951, the year he received a prestigious national literary award for his novella *The Wall: The Crime of S. Karuma*, he was a zealous Marxist activist and a prolific writer of surrealistic tales, many of which centered around the theme of metamorphosis. His 1962 novel *Woman in the Dunes*, a nightmarish fable whose film version won the Jury Prize at the 1964 Cannes Film Festival, established his literary reputation on an international scale. Although Abe never practiced medicine, his scientific training is evident in the minute descriptions of material phenomena and the cool, clinical tone that characterize his fiction. Probably no other Japanese writer has managed to capture such wildly imaginative fantasies in a prose style that suggests naturalistic verisimilitude.

The typical protagonist of Abe's stories is an "outsider" who is haunted by a sense of alienation and by anxiety over the fragility of individual identity. He seeks freedom from the oppressiveness of communal reality, yet yearns futilely for emotional connection. These universal themes, combined with the ironical manner of their expression, have prompted many to remark that Abe's work bears a closer resemblance to that of certain western writers, notably Kafka, than to traditional Japanese literary models. Yet Abe's fiction reflects its native heritage through its vividly imagistic prose, its abundant incorporation of Japanese cultural icons, and its satirical treatment of Japanese psychosocial dynamics.

Although he is known chiefly as a novelist, Abe was a skilled playwright, photographer, and essayist as well. His theatrical achievements were especially significant. He founded an acting studio in Tokyo in 1973, where he trained performers in his innovative performance methods and directed plays. Abe died in 1993, while still vigorously engaged in various creative pursuits.

a note on the type

This book was set in Caledonia, a Linotype face designed by W. A. Dwiggins (1880–1956). It belongs to the family of printing types called "modern face" by printers—a term used to mark the change in style of type letters that occurred about 1800.

Caledonia borders on the general design of Scotch Roman, but is more freely drawn than that letter.

Composed by PennSet, Bloomsburg, Pennsylvania
Printed and bound by The Haddon Craftsmen, Scranton, Pennsylvania
Designed by Iris Weinstein